Moonpool

By

Kingsley Taylor

Grosvenor House
Publishing Limited

This book is published by
Grosvenor House Publishing Ltd
Link House
140 The Broadway, Tolworth, Surrey, KT6 7HT.
www.grosvenorhousepublishing.co.uk

A CIP record for this book
is available from the British Library

ISBN 978-1-83975-817-1

Dedication

To Joanne, great, great, ...

... great, great, granddaughter of Little Rainbow

To Jonathan &

[illegible]

Believe

[illegible]

Preface

Some years ago I took an MA in Celtic Christianity at Lampeter College, for my dissertation I did the history of the Group of parishes I am Vicar of from the end of the Roman Occupation to the beginning of the Middle Ages. While researching this I found so much archaeological evidence of earlier times, so I continued doing research back to the end of the last ice age, 10,000 years ago. I wanted to write a novel based on the development of people from the earliest settlers, but how to do this? I discovered St Mary's Church is built in an elliptical enclosure (or a henge) in line with the rising sun of the equinox. Early one equinox morning I watched the sun rise to check the alignment, the penny dropped, I met Moonpool and this then is her story.

Contents

Chapter 1

Perceptions

My perceptions changed when the first human came to my lake and just stood. I had heard of them but until then I had not seen one. This creature didn't drink but just stood gazing. I could not understand why it just stood there, was it waiting for something or was something going on in its inner being? But I realised I was waiting too, and this surprised me because I had no perception of time until that moment.

I had witnessed The Maker Of All Things bring the cosmic forces and matter together in this corner of the galaxy, I has seen the small star that was to provide light here being formed and the smaller bodies that surrounded it. I was brought down onto this one and saw that which was to be the Moon smashed off from it, I saw the rocks cool, the waters spread, and growing things appear on the land. I saw life begin and the creatures that roamed about develop and die and develop again. I was here as the ice came and went many times over the land I was given to protect and I watched as a valley was carved and filled with a lake, a place of beauty and peace.

I watched as the red deer came roaming over the grassy plains. They came and drank in the lake and grazed on the hills. They moved with the cycle of the seasons, further east through the cold winter and the long dark nights. I watched them coming again with their young in the early spring and the lengthening of the days. I watched them graze and drink before they moved on into the mountains for the long warm summer and the long days. I watched them come again in the autumn, the stag mating with the doe, their breath misting in the cooler air before they left again to the east.

Fish began to teem in the waters of the lake, so many forms, swimming up the river and with great effort ascending the waterfall to spawn and then back to feed. And there were the birds as they watched the fish and as it is in nature catching and feeding on them.

Yet the passing of time was something I did not understand and still find difficult to completely come to terms with.

But this being stood and gazed. It was such a small time, practically no time at all, yet I found myself waiting.

I looked in its eyes and there was intelligence and reflection of a depth I had never seen in a creature before, and I was curious.

I saw that it actually had very little hair itself, on its head and round the lower part of its face but what it had on the rest of its body was quite sparse, rather it was wearing the skin and hair of another creature, the red deer, and this shocked me for a moment. I had seen creatures kill others for food; it was part of the natural order of life, but never before for their skins. I also wondered at this because it did not have dangerous claws or teeth, how could such a frail and defenceless creature be a killer. I saw that it did have in its hand a long straight stick with a sharpened stone bound onto the end, it also had a piece of antler sharpened into an edge tucked into a band at its waist. Here was a creature capable of making tools to hunt.

I knew the form, or more specifically a similar form. Many of our kind can take on this form and I wondered that a creature had been given this gift as what was presumably its normal form. I took on the form myself but in a vague, shifting way, for I was as yet unused to it and wasn't sure how I should appear, and I stood behind the creature.

From his perspective, for I knew now in this form that it was a male, I could see what he gazed so intently at. It was night and the stars and the Moon were reflected in my still waters, but it was at the reflected Moon that he gazed. Why did he gaze at her reflection so intently rather than directly at her? Did he think this was a second Moon, perhaps one he could reach? Would he dive into the water to catch her?

I was aware of so much more because of the senses I now had. I could feel the cold of the night air, the slumbering breaths of the sleeping creatures and the stealthy movements of those that were awake. I could see the lights in the sky as the bodies those of my kind dwelt in, and the Moon in her mysterious sphere so near yet so far, so cold yet so vital. I smelt the earth, and the growing plants and felt the grass under my feet. There was no breeze and the surface of my lake was still like crystal. The light of the Moon gave a pale glow to all the land and it wasn't until later that I realised that it must have given a dreamlike quality to everything from the man's perspective.

I could hear the slow steady breathing of the man and the strong beat of his mortal heart. He was alone and still and the world around him was quiet. He seemed to be almost lost in a dream.

He drew in a breath and let it out slowly. Then he uttered sounds. These were not the sounds of any other creature I had ever heard, there was meaning in them that I couldn't quite grasp. Only later would I understand that he had just named my lake and therefore also me, and in the language that you, the reader, would understand he said, "Moonpool."

"Moonpool." I repeated the sounds as sounds only, not aware of the meaning at that point. Yet in a strange way it cut to the very depths of my being and my form settled, my hair became dark almost as the night itself, my skin pale as the Moon, my eyes blue and deep as the still waters, my raiment silver at my shoulders fading to a deep, deep blue below my knees, my feet were bare.

He gave a start but did not run. I have seen so many creatures run after such a start, sensing danger. But in his surprise he must have reasoned there was no danger, only the sounds he had uttered being repeated back to him. Slowly he turned and saw me in the form I had taken. He gazed at me for some time, turned back to look at my lake and turned back to me again. He blinked and wiped his free hand across his eyes and looked intently at me again.

"Moonpool?" He said to me with a questioning look in his eye.

I realised that the sounds meant something that referred to me, perhaps a name, so I was amazed at the connection he had made between my physical form and the lake. This was a creature of intelligence and understanding.

"Moonpool." I repeated back to him again beginning to realise the implication of the sounds.

"Ban." He tapped his chest.

"Ban." I repeated the sounds.

"Moonpool." He extended his free hand toward me, and, "Ban." He tapped his chest.

I really understood now.

He nodded his head and I nodded mine. He widened his mouth into what I later understood to be a smile and I copied the expression.

He pointed up at the orb in the sky. "Moon."

He turned to my lake and back to me again stretched his arm back towards my lake.

"Moonpool?"

I nodded. He had made a distinction between the Moon and her reflection and had made the connection between the physical form I had taken for a while and my lake, though I had no idea how he had made this connection. There must be something in my appearance that spoke to him of my lake and the reflection of the Moon, this pleased me because I am so much less than the Moon and hold her in reverence.

He turned back towards my lake. Took his stick in both hands, broke it across his knee and threw it into my lake, disturbing the reflected Moon in the ripples. Then he turned to me, knelt down with his head bowed and spoke again words I did not understand. He paused, stood up and strode away up over the hill and out of sight.

"Ban." I called but knew none of his words to stop him.

I was curious but for a while I did nothing, perhaps I should have followed him but somehow I felt it would be wrong for me to go to him, rather it was his place to come to me.

In the depths of my lake the half of the stick that had the sharpened stone of flint sank. This weapon must have taken some time and effort to make and I couldn't understand why he had simply cast it away, unless ... I dare not think.

Chapter 2

Settlement

The Earth spun in the vastness of space in the great dance that is the universe. The deer moved back and forth across the land that had become my home. For a while my lake froze over while the tilt of the Earth brought the longer nights and as the days lengthened thawed again. Many dormant plants began to shoot again as the sunlight gained in strength.

Ban returned and two men were with him, this time it was day. They strode over the hill down to my shore; Ban's companions were shorter and followed slightly behind him. They stopped near the shore of the lake and knelt down with their heads bowed. Ban spoke but I had not yet gained the knowledge of the sounds apart from the one word "Moonpool." Then they stood up.

For a while they just stood and gazed across the lake, were they waiting for something? Were they waiting for a response from me? For the second time in my long existence I waited too. Should I appear to them? Somehow I didn't feel I could. Had Ban been on his own maybe but even then I wouldn't have felt it was right. I had given in to curiosity before but I was unsure what I was supposed to do, I was the spirit not just of the lake but of the valley and as such I had a responsibility for the animals that came there but whether I should interact with them hadn't been revealed to me.

They stepped back to a fairly level place some distance from the lake where they removed bundles of skins and firs they had brought with them on their backs. I was enthralled as they drew out of the bundles some dry pieces of wood and dried grasses, long sticks and deer hides. One of the companions made a sort of nest of stones he gathered from the shore of the lake, dried grasses and fragments of wood, he started rapidly turning one piece of wood between his hands against another. Ban and the other placed two long sticks into the ground, unfolded a large hide and pulled the end over the sticks to form a shelter.

Suddenly there was a spark from the wood and dried grasses and the first companion soon has a fire going and carefully placed more of the dry wood on it.

Ban and the second man came to the lake again, bowed, turned and strode off both with a long stick with a sharpened stone bound on one end.

The man with the fire stayed, he had brought quite a stock of wood with him which he laid down near the fire. Then he came and stood by my lake again, he had a long piece of deer antler that had barbs carved down one side.

"Moonpool." He said, and here you must bear with me because the language these men spoke is a long lost language now even if related to a language still used and I must do my best in the language you know to describe the words I began to pick up. "Beg" was one word that had been used by Ban and this man and "I" seemed to be a general word they used for themselves rather than an individual name. The general meaning I presume was that he was asking for something from me.

As a sort of trial I caused a large trout to swim perilously near to him. Quick as a flash the antler was in the fish, he lifted it out and put it on the grass. The man bowed and tapped his chest.

"Storr." He said. Then at a rough guess, "Thank you."

He picked up the fish and took it back to the fire. Using another sharpened piece of antler he cut open the fish and removed its inwards which he dug a hole for and buried, he then placed the fish on a short stick and planted the other end in the ground so the fish was suspended over the fire.

A while later Ban and the other man came back over the hill carrying part of the body of a deer. They approached the lake, bowed, and went to join Storr.

I watched as the Earth turned through night and day many times. Sometimes I would bring a fish to Storr, sometimes he would disappear for a while and return with more wood for the fire. Ban and the other man whose name I never learned skinned the parts of the deer they would hunt, scraping them with a short piece of bone with a sharpened end, pegging out the skins to dry in the sun. The three of them would feast on the fish and deer they cooked over the fire and drank from a small stream that flowed into my lake but never from the lake itself. They had a skin they had sewed together that seemed to hold a quantity of water without leaking too much which they would fill with water from a nearby stream to bring back to the camp and take with them if they were away from the camp.

In all this time I didn't appear to them, but watched and learned, slowly I came to understand much of what they were saying to each other.

It became obvious that their stay was only temporary and they spoke about hunting somewhere else. Then, one morning with the lengthening of the days and the moving of the deer to the mountains they put out the fire, rolled up their shelter and packed all their things together, by now they had a sizeable pack of skins as well.

"The two of you go ahead," Said Ban as they shouldered their packs, "I must say my thanks."

He watched them go over the hill then turned to my lake.

"Moonpool. I thank you for your .. (a word I didn't know) and for all you have given us."

He raised his spear and was about to break it over his knee when without even thinking I stood before him to stop him. The suddenness of my appearance startled him.

"There is no need for that." I said to him. "I cannot use it and do not need it. I have had much from you that you do not know."

He lowered his eyes because he couldn't look directly at me for long. He was about to kneel.

"Ban, don't." I said. Some of the things I needed to say I hadn't the words for yet.

Still, he remained standing. He rested the end of his spear on the ground and paused for a moment.

"I must go." He said almost apologetically. "There are .. (another unknown word) to do then I must return to .. (?), but I will be back."

This human form can be so uncomfortable and confusing at times, at that moment I had to leave it and withdraw to the peace of the lake and the spinning of the world. I didn't see him go.

"O Maker Of All Things, what is this confusion, what are these feelings."

"Do not do anything in haste. Do not think these feelings are anything more than they are. You are one and he is another. Experience what there is but go no further."

"I do not understand."

"When you do, remember what I say."

"Should I not appear to them then? Should I keep my distance? You haven't told me what you expect of me in this place."

"This is still a young people and they may yet need your help."

And this was the best I was going to get as an answer.

So the world rolled on, the Sun rose and fell, the deer passed by again but the men did not come, the days grew short and cold, the lake froze over though the ice was not so thick now, the land was still, the Sun sank to his lowest and was reborn again, the ice melted, the deer came with their young. I was calm.

A group of people came over the hill. Ban and Storr were among them but not the other man who had come the last time, there were also two other men and two women. Of the two new men, one had hair that was turning white and the other had no beard on his face. One of the women had a lined face and her lank hair was streaked with grey, the other seemed fresh and young and nervous like a young deer. They came to the lake.

"Moonpool." Ban began, paused. He continued. "I beg we may have safety here, I ask your .. (a word I didn't know). We are your (?)"

The older woman took a cord strung with small bones and animal teeth from her neck and threw it into the lake. I watched it as it sank slowly, a cord of rushes plaited together, small ankle bones and teeth from a deer had been drilled through and threaded onto the cord. I could see no purpose in it, was it a mark of conquests or simply an adornment? I let it sink.

"We pay you .. (?)." She said in a thin, quavering voice.

With that they settled on the flat stretch of ground that they had camped on before. Storr built a fire and Ban and the younger man began to erect a shelter, larger than before that was enclosed on three sides, open only towards my lake, the two older people unrolled firs and lay them inside the shelter and lay out an array of wooden bowls. All this time the younger woman gazed across my surface deep in thought. I knew she was hoping to see me and I wondered what Ban had told her.

"What is your name?" I whispered to her and her alone.

"Lia." She whispered back. "Are you Moonpool?"

"So Ban named me."

"Can I see you?"

"You are seeing me."

She looked puzzled, narrowed her eyes a little, gazed out over my lake, and finally shook her head.

"No, I can't"

"There is no need."

Her need to see me was more than simple curiosity but I was not inclined to appear. Besides I don't think she was quite sure enough of my existence and wasn't convinced that the words I spoke to here were her own imagination.

The shelter was very slow in going up, this wasn't because of its size but that Ban was constantly looking over at Lia. He had a very odd, hungry look in his eyes. I had seen this look in the eyes of stag but never so intense. What I found slightly disturbing was that it was almost as if the intelligence in Ban's eyes had drained away. Then, because Lia was standing by my lake Ban's gaze would sweep over the surface, he would remember himself and concentrate on the shelter for a while.

The Sun sank low to the horizon before the camp was all settled; pieces of meat were hung over the fire and the company sat around the fire and only then started to talk. And as they talked I learned more of their language.

They talked of their home in the far south, they talked of the richness of this land that they didn't have to share with anyone else and the herds of red deer, they talked of either staying or moving on and they talked of me and my provision and protection.

Ban stood, lightly touched Lia on the shoulder so she stood as well. I knew what this was but what they did next rather surprised me. They approached the lake and knelt down together.

"Moonpool, provider of all things, this night bless our coming together and provide us with a child." Said Ban.

The Moon was high above, she had been asked for this same blessing many times and it was not as if I needed her permission but she is greater than me and

I only reflect her so I asked. Though her face didn't change I knew that she was touched that this should be asked of me and that I would defer to her and so I knew she was happy with this. I caused a ripple on the surface of my lake, enough to make her reflection dance in the eyes of the humans but not to break her image.

"Moonpool, can I see you?" Asked Lia.

She took a strip of leather from her neck that had a very smooth stone with a hole bored in it fastened to the leather strip; then she threw it far out into my lake. As it sank I noted that the stone had been smoothed by the waves of the sea on a distant shore. I still did not feel it was right to appear, I had given all the answer I needed and this was her time, hers and Ban's and I would not intrude at this special time for them.

These creatures are animals the same as all other animals in their nature and I saw the animal need in both of them, yet this extra gift that they have of intelligence and understanding and the powerful bond of love was a thing I couldn't yet fully grasp.

They stood and paused for a moment before walking back to the shelter where they came together in the most beautiful act that nature is, I saw in this both the animal and the higher emotion of love. This was not just an act of lust for the procreation of young but a coming together of two souls. The others in the group remained by the fire, talking together in hushed tones.

Chapter 3

Growth

Lia would often come to me at night. She would stand and gaze across the lake and, when the sky was clear and full of stars I wondered if she could hear them singing. The Moon rose high in the sky and Lia would gaze at the Moon's reflection. The Moon passed from full to half and came later in the night. In all this time the weather was calm and dry, and barely a breeze troubled the surface of the lake. Lia would talk about Ban and about the child she hoped was growing within her. And she waited.

"All is well." I would whisper to her, for I knew the child had already begun and I would do everything in my power to help and protect. But I had decided I would appear to none of them so as not to interfere with their lives and their development. If they needed me I was here and that was enough.

After many days the Moon now fully waned and a new Moon had begun. The humans had gathered a stock of skins and antlers and bones. Then Ban and Storr packed some things together for a journey, took up the things they had gathered, and then they turned to the lake.

"Moonpool," Said Ban, "I humbly ask that you would bless our journey, keep us safe and bring us success. I would also ask that you would look after the camp and particularly take care of Lia for me."

He took the antler tool from his belt and threw it into the lake. I could not do anything about their journey except ask my brothers and sisters to watch out for them, but Ban knew I would protect the others who remained.

The older woman, whose name was Shana, tended to Lia, she reassured her and prepared a drink with herbs for her every time the Sun was about to sink beyond the horizon. Both of them would dig in the ground for roots along the bank of the nearest river to them that brought the water to me from the hills.

They had a store of dried meat so there was no need to hunt. The older man, called Har, taught the younger, called Tan, to fish and they were most careful to thank me every time I caused a fish to move towards them.

I realised I was waiting again even without taking on physical form. I was caught up in the small lives of a group of humans which in the order of things would pass unnoticed. But I was drawn in to their sense of passing time, every time the Sun rose and strode across the sky to sink in the west was important to them.

I was almost ready to appear at least to Lia, but I was still unsure of the feelings I had last time I took physical form. I waited while the Moon went past the full waned and waxed again, perhaps when she was at her fullest and all her glory reflected in my waters and then, perhaps, I might.

But the day before she was at her fullest again Ban and Storr returned and with them was a group of people, five and five and five. Mostly men, broad and strong, some women and two smaller people, these were young children, the first I had seen.

They brought spears and knives, large quantities of wood and shaped antler tools. They drove poles into the ground and started weaving thinner wood between them.

Some of the men, led by Ban, would go off to hunt while others would go back down the valley and bring back more wood and dried grasses.

The dwelling took shape, a large circular hut of poles and covered with skins. This was obviously a permanent shelter, it seemed they intended to stay and I was glad.

Each night Ban and Lia would come and sit by the lake for a while and talk of their hopes and fears for the future and the children that would follow. They would ask for my blessing and then lay together under the original shelter. Others of the group were paired as well, but they had been together some time already and the two children were obviously from these unions.

But it was the children that I found most interesting, two boys they were, they would run, they would pretend to hunt each other, and they would wrestle. The taller would always win. Tam and Sett. They were not brothers, Tam was tall and broad, very strong but not very fast, Sett was thin and much faster, and he was the brighter of the two.

One evening as the Sun was slowly sinking in the west they were grappling with each other. Tam out of pure muscle pulled Sett to the ground and attempt to sit on him with all his weight, but Sett being so much more agile managed to slip from his grasp, but as he tried to stand he lost his balance and rolled down the slope into the lake. The water was already quite deep at this point and it never occurred to me that he couldn't swim, all animals swim and these humans were just as buoyant and capable of swimming. He splashed about and I felt his panic deep within me, it was this panic that kept him from swimming. Tam ran down after him and began to wade out to him, up to just above his knees, but I could feel his fear as he froze to the spot unable to go further and not far enough to reach Sett.

"Sett! Sett! Help! Help!" He called.

Two of the men and one of the women who were at the camp began to run. I could feel the water entering Sett's lungs, I felt him getting weaker. Do I intervene? Do I let nature take its course, accidents happen, animals drown, such is the way of life but this was a human animal and would the others understand if I simply let him drown. The camp was just too far and Sett had so little time. I didn't really think about it, I lifted him with my arms and lay him gently on the pebbles on the shore, I lay my hand on his chest to be sure his heart still beat and his lungs drew breath. When I was sure, then I looked up, the woman took him in her arms and all three got down on their knees facing me a mixture of fear, gratitude and wonder in their eyes. Tam stood where he was in the water trembling with fright unwilling even to turn and look at us on the shore.

I retreated, this had been on impulse and I was not sure that I should have got involved. There is a place in the depths of the lake, not quite at the deepest but very near the centre. It is a place where the veil between the physical world and the real world is very thin, a place where I can meet with my brothers and sister without having to leave the lake.

"You have grown, my daughter." Said Silverwheel.

"Too quickly."

"Quickly? You know nothing of time."

"Watching these humans has taught me something of time but with them time is long."

"Because they are mortal and their time is short in the order of things. Every time the Sun is in the sky is important to them and so to them it is long, but that is all they have."

"Sett would have had no time at all if I hadn't saved him, was I wrong to do so?"

"There is no right or wrong only good or evil, but you must understand The Maker Of All Things has gifted them with a dual being and only Sett's physical being would have ended. What you did was a comfort for the community who live with you especially his parents because they do not know their duality and cannot see beyond their mortal lives. The reaction of the people to you and your response to them will determine whether it was good or evil. You meant only good and that is the best way to start."

"Then how should I respond?"

"I have seen these beings all round the world for a lot longer than you and even now I cannot predict how they will respond. Ban is wise for a mortal, talk to him. He understands his people very well."

North from the camp the ground rises to a small hill, not the highest in the area but close enough to have a good view of the greater part of the lake. It was deep night and there was no Moon in the sky, clouds scudded across alternately revealing and obscuring the stars. I called to Ban in the whisper of the breeze and by the light of the visible stars he came quietly without rousing even Lia.

He kneeled to me and I sat down facing slightly away from him. I knew he was looking intently at me, somewhat confused. So I patted the ground beside me.

"I am not your equal." He said.

"No, you are not." I patted the ground again.

Slowly he stood then sat beside me facing across the lake. If only the Moon had been in the sky, but this felt like it was a test. He clasped and unclasped his hands for some time, this was the first time we had met for many turns of the earth and the first where we had just sat.

"We are not equal as you say." I said. "Yet I have learned much from your people that I didn't know as spirit. Still there is much I do not know. I would learn your thoughts at this time."

"You saved Sett and gave him back life. We owe you so much already how can we ever repay you."

"Sett was not dead and I cannot give life, I saved him from drowning only. As I said I have learned much from you and your people we help each other, talk not of repayment."

"But we impose on you, camping where we do."

"You have to camp somewhere and all land and water is overseen, if you see this as imposing then you will impose on some spirit wherever you are. We are guardians only and The Maker Of All Things has given you the land to settle and grow."

"I still fear we impose on you, perhaps in some way … but I know no stronger words to express my fear. For you are goddess."

"Why do you not drink from the lake, why walk all the way over there for water."

"The lake is you."

"What of the sprite of the river? Do you not fear to impose on her?"

"I didn't know there was one, I never saw her."

"All land and water is overseen."

"This hill?" He patted the ground.

"This is still me, and the hills across there, all the valley, I am not just the lake."

He was silent for a long time.

"We have both grown, have we not?" I said. "Your child grows too."

I heard him gasp, his heart almost miss a beat.

"You are a wise man Ban, you make a good leader, and you will make a good father."

He bowed his head to his knees.

"Tell me, Ban, how do the others think of me?"

"You are goddess, to see you frightens them but also they are glad that you are here looking over them. You saved Sett and they are glad, yet they still fear you because we always fear what we do not understand."

"Then I should not take this form."

"Humans forget easily, it would be well to remind us from time to time. They also get too familiar, don't appear often. Balance is important and who can really tell where this is."

"You have not become familiar."

"What we have is complicated, I'm sure you see that. I am human, you are goddess and we must leave it there. Also we each have our responsibilities."

"You are a wise man Ban. I will watch over Lia and the child."

Ban was also a very open man in his thoughts. I saw that the night he first came to the lake and saw the Moon reflected in the water he had been dreaming a sort of waking dream. When he uttered the first word I ever heard he was not only speaking of the what he saw but an image in his head, I became that image and when he turned and saw me it was no wonder he was drawn to me. Yet he has the sense to realise the difference between his world and mine, his dream and reality. I understood now why he left so abruptly and never returned alone. But how did I feel, he was the first human I ever met and until I took on this form I had no feelings at all. I may be older than the world itself but there are times I feel young as if I know nothing.

We sat and said nothing for a while. Then Ban rose and bowed low to me.

"My goddess and my friend."

With that he retreated down the hill.

I sat for some time longer enjoying the sights, sounds and smells of the physical world. I reflected on Ban's passing remark, no nearer understanding humanity at all.

Chapter 4

Winter

As the deer travelled into the mountains Ban led five and two men and three women after them. Har and Shana he left in charge of the camp.

Shana would often come to the lake at night and stand and gaze even though the clouds had rolled in and all was dark, even when the wind blew from the east. She didn't speak. I could see deep wisdom in her face. I still had no conception of time and how important it was for these people but I knew she felt she was getting closer to her end and I wondered that it bothered her so little. She was so calm. I found these periods of stillness with her on the shore quite intimate, as if it was just the two of us enjoying each other's company though we were so different. She was an open person and I could tell she was aware of my presence, I could have appeared to her but that was not necessary for either of us.

Tam and Sett kept well away from the lake, casting a suspicious glance towards it every now and then, some of the innocent fun had gone from them and Tam particularly had become withdrawn and sullen. Yet they were still close to each other. They both had long sticks with which they tried to catch hares. Every day Lia collected wild flowers and reeds from the banks of the rivers running into the lake; she wove them together and cast them onto the surface of the lake. Storr continued to catch fish in my lake but now he was so good at it I didn't need to nudge them towards him. He would always bow to me before he did so and again after he caught something, once he threw the barbed antler far into the lake as an offering to me and had to select and carve another one. So the camp survived on fish, dried deer meat, the occasional hare, herbs and roots.

The days grew long then began to shorten again. In time Ban returned with his companions. They had a quantity of deer skins, antlers and dried meat. Much of what they had two of the men and one of the women took away to the east.

Ban noticed that Lia now showed visible signs of the child growing within her and he fussed over her. I had not seen him so gentle and caring before. That evening as the sun began to set in the west they came to the bank of the lake and sat.

"Moonpool." Said Ban. "Thank you for watching over Lia and the others. We have a good store of food and hope to winter here since I do not want Lia to travel. Watch over us this winter and I ask that you make it a mild winter." He thought for a while then continued. "If the child is a girl I will call her Moonpool so I will apologise if it is a boy."

But I knew it was a boy already, this I kept to myself, let it be a surprise.

The deer moved east, the sun sank lower in the sky. The air grew cooler and the days shorter. Some of the men made several trips to get wood until they had a good stock ready for the winter.

As yet only small bushes grew in the valleys, no trees had yet come to this area and there was very little here of any use for fire or tools. Some of the pebbles on the shore of the lake could be chipped enough to make a rough scraping tool and some large enough to be bored through with patience and attached to a wooden handle but there was none of the flint that could be made sharp enough for their spears.

So it was with great joy that the group who had taken the skins away returned with new spears fastened with stones to replace ones they had lost or broken in the mountains. They had also brought enough materials for a second dwelling which they all set too to build before the winter really took hold.

The year marched on towards midwinter and the group huddled together closer about the fire, they told stories of the hunt in the mountains and of the people towards the east and south that they traded with. They told stories of some of my kind and their dealings with the humans, many of which I knew not to be true and I could see that these people were somewhat frightened of us. These people actually knew very little of the world as it really was and had made stories to explain why the sun came and went, why the Moon waxed and waned. They had stories about how the world had begun which involved a goddess who gave birth to everything, about wars in the higher realm which did have some basis in the truth which is why there is always chaos and order and why it was best for them to be a little wary of us.

The shortest day came, not as cold as other years for the lake was not freezing over, yet this was not my doing it was the change in the climate as the ice retreated further and further north. They piled much of their stock of wood on the fire that night and sat around it holding vigil and chanting. They chanted words of power so that the Sun might be born again. I quietly sat among them while they were so intent that I managed to do so unnoticed. It was unwise of them, especially Lia, to be out at night in the cold so I created a slight warming of the air about them. The chanting was powerful and moving. Even though I knew he would rise again, and I suspected that these people all knew it too, and it was probably the same all over this part of the world, it was still magical and I am sure the Sun was honoured.

As dawn approached and the sky began to lighten perceptibly the excitement grew, we all stood and began to dance round the fire; there was real power in their collective fervent prayer. The light grew and grew in the east and a shout went up as the edge of the Sun broke over the hillside.

A hand was laid on my shoulder. I turned.

"Thank you for sharing this with us." Said Ban. "You know you are always welcome, but some of them fear you and not all are peaceful. Go now, before they see."

I went to my thin place and sought Light of the Long Hand.

"That was an interesting event to be part of, I suppose you were honoured by it."

"I always am, though we both know this is simply the natural cycle of the world. I often wonder what is in the minds of the humans though; do they really believe I have died? You are closer to them, perhaps one day you can find out."

"I think they know really, they are not stupid. But why do mortals fear us and what is meant by not all are peaceful?"

"There is a certain pride in humans I have seen all over the world. They acknowledge us and, as you saw, worship us. Yet few would be willing to meet with us for we remind them of their fragility and powerlessness and the shortness of their lives. Your Ban is an interesting exception. There are those who want to believe they can do without us and there are some who would destroy us if they could to prove they are the masters. Do not get too close, it is tempting because they live in the moment and there is an attraction in that. Some of us have fallen and lived among them but nothing ever good has come from it. We are not meant to live in the moment, we are guardians. You are a peaceful spirit and you endow the valley with peace, without you where would these people be? I cannot say."

"Do they really need us?"

He thought for a moment. "They are a strange race, both animal and spirit and The Maker Of All Things does have a plan and a special place in his heart for them. He cannot reveal all to them in one go, they are still young and the first to have that level of intelligence. Let them believe in us for the moment, it is as much as they can understand for now."

The shortest day had come and gone yet the winter had a long way to go for the humans for it is after the shortest day that the weather is at its coldest. The food store was visibly depleting and some of it was beginning to rot. The lake still didn't freeze over and there was only the occasional dusting of snow but there were few animals about and nothing much was growing. They found roots in the marshy ground where rivers came to the lake, the occasional hare who ventured out early and there were still fish in the lake. Lia was getting near her time and Ban was very worried and attentive to her. Shana calmly tended to her and made sure she ate often going without food herself.

It rained steadily for several days and the fires were started in the huts as it was impossible to keep the one outside dry. A cold wind blew from the north and although many mornings the frost lay on the ground the lake still didn't freeze. Apart from several of the men going out to hunt for whatever they could find there was little movement outside the huts.

One night when the Moon was full the clouds rolled away she shone brightly and the entire camp left their shelter wrapped warmly in skins and came down to the shore where they had the full benefit of her reflection in my lakes still surface. Lia was very near her time now, she had carved a figure out of antler and she tossed it far out into the lake. As it slowly sank I tried to make out what it was in the likeness of, it was roughly human in shape but it was curled up, coming from Lia I took it to be a baby and she was hoping I would help in some way with the birth of her child.

"Moonpool." Said Ban. "Protect Lia in the coming days and protect our unborn child. Bring the deer back so we do not starve for we have little food left. We will give you whatever you ask. Look over us all now because life has become hard."

I was aware that the time of year was almost upon us when the deer did return, the young would be born and their mothers would be full of milk but this was not my doing. Yet Ban would believe it was and I could not help this. Lia was young and healthy and strong so her chances were good and I would help as much as I could but life and death are not mine to choose. The Maker Of All Things had brought these people here for a reason so I felt fairly confident that all would be well. So I brought the little figure back to the shore.

Lia saw it faintly white in the moonlight against the dark of the water. She reached down and picked it out of the water, clutching it to her bosom her eyes filled with tears. “Thank you, Moonpool, oh thank you.”

Chapter 5

Stirrings

There is a time when, although the winter hasn't finished with the land, there is the early stirring of spring. The doe are in milk and the young are born. A time when they start to move back to the higher land, they were now nearer to the valley, close enough for the hunters to get fresh meat. And so it was on this day that Lia went into labour. A day when the sky was blue and clear and the sun shone and there was a light frost on the grass which quickly melted away.

Har came to the lake and waited, gazing across the lake. What his thoughts were I could not guess, some people are open in their thoughts but he was not. Through all that followed he stood and waited, holding some sort of vigil.

All the occupants of one of the huts were pushed out so only Shena and Lia were left. Ban ran back and forth for dry, clean skins and for clean water which for once he took from the lake in the sewn skin he used.

Quietly I sat with Lia, Shana glanced up and smiled. "Hold her hand Moonpool. Anything else that is in your power I pray you do for her."

I held her hand and I channelled peace and strength. I could feel the child, he was strong and the right way round but if anything a little large for Lia's small frame. So I took some of her pain and by my very nature was able to reach within her and I relaxed her and helped her as she pushed. If my hand had been a human hand she could have squeezed the blood out of it but even in human form I have the strength of rock and soil.

She pushed and, cold as it was outside, she was drenched in sweat, she screamed out and the child's head emerged. She pushed and screamed again and the small shoulders emerged, Shana pulled the small body and Lia pushed again and he was born. Lia was bleeding but that I could help with too. I stayed long enough to see the joy in both of the women, to hear the boy cry and to watch Shana tie the cord then I released Lia's hand and left quietly. I had seen this so many times in the creatures that roamed the land but this was special, the first human birth, new life of a being that was both flesh and spirit.

Ban was filling the skin with water when he heard the boy cry and he ran back up to the hut, nearly falling with his impatience. He went in and the rest of the camp crowded round to wait. Ban emerged and proudly held up his son to show him off.

"Rab son of Ban. He will be a great hunter." He strode down to the lake and said again. "Rab son of Ban. He will be a great hunter."

"Ban." Shouted Shana. "Bring the boy back, it is cold, the shock will kill him, bring him back."

Another place I found was a good place to sit while in mortal form was at the edge of the lake where it emptied out over a series of waterfalls and at the right time of day the sun would cause little rainbows to play in the mist. There I would sit with Little Rainbow the sprite of the falls and chat about the doings of the humans. She had never seen them up close because they never came this way but had seen the occasional hunter further down the valley.

I needed someone to share this experience with.

"These mortals, they seem so big and clumsy." She said.

"They would to you."

"What of your people? I know you, you have some news."

"Lia has just given birth, as babies they are so defenceless. The young deer begin to walk soon after they are born but human babies cannot. You know they have very little hair of their own; they have no protection against the cold."

"I would have liked to see this."

"You know you are free to roam within the valley, you could have come."

"I feel safe here, I am not sure of these humans. Tell me about the baby."

"We have both seen animals give birth, but this was so different. These humans are so much more than animals, this new baby will grow to understand many things but he is so helpless now and will be for quite some time."

"You want to protect this baby don't you, and more than just as guardian."

"We are one and they are another."

"But still, in this form we have feelings we do not understand."

"And I know we shouldn't."

"I hear tales coming up the river. It is possible for us to mate with them. Though what any of us would want to do that for I do not know, perhaps you would know better than me."

"I have heard these things too. It seems only sorrow comes of this because their time is so short." And in a way I envied them, I felt I was missing something by not living in the present with the urgency of time.

We just sat for a while. From there we could see a long way down the valley. It was quiet, only a few small animals had begun to stir this early in the year.

"I don't know about you, Little Rainbow, but I still do not understand time."

"Nor I. I will always be young and I will always play." With that she skipped away and was one with the water.

There was still much of the winter to come but at least the herds had returned and the hunters were able to hunt for fresh meat. I deliberately kept away from Lia and the baby and I avoided taking on human form because it was like an empty yearning within me.

The rains fell and the wind blew cold from the west for a while but the humans got through the winter and as long as future winters were not harsh the camp was now here for good. Time would pass and I would watch over them as they developed and learned. Yet I would have to keep my distance and avoid taking on human form because in that form it was too tempting to be part of them and live a human life. And yet, even in spirit form, communing with my own kind, I could feel the pull of the humans.

Chapter 6

Development

The seasons came and went, the earth went round the Sun, the winters grew milder and trees began to spread from the valley beyond the waterfall into my valley and up into the hills. The boy, Rab, grew and the other boys began to take an interest in him. Ban and Lia had a daughter who they named Moonpool as promised. Two other children were born in the camp and a third hut was built. Some of the men and women would go into the mountains in the summer to hunt and take the skins and antlers into the east in the autumn.

Lia would often bring Moonpool to the lake, as soon as she was able to stand Moonpool would stand with her mother and they would both wait and gaze across the waters. On a clear day when the breeze ruffled the surface of the lake the light of the sun would dance and sparkle and Moonpool would laugh. Moonpool was a very open girl in her thoughts and would try and imagine what I looked like in my physical form, she was quite accurate yet I never appeared to her.

Moonpool grew into a fast and agile girl. One autumn the traders returned with a new weapon, short, light sticks with small sharpened stones fastened on one end and feathers on the other, these they could hurl at animals with a long flexible stick tied with animal gut, a bow and arrows. Moonpool took to this very quickly and was soon shooting birds out of the sky. She was much better with this than any of the others. She had a keen eye and saw where to shoot ahead of the bird so bird and arrow arrived together.

Shana became feeble and the day she died there was a great deal of weeping in the camp. They carried her body up into the hills at the very edge of the valley chanting and lay her there. Lia had woven a garland with flowers and reeds which she laid on Shana's body. They called on Light of the Long Hand to take her life force and quietly moved away leaving the birds to peck her flesh from her bones. Many days later they went up the hill and brought her bones back laying them carefully in the first and largest hut and covering them with reeds from the marsh. Lia would often sit with the bones and talk to Shana as if she could still hear. Life and death is so much part of nature in the physical world and it fascinated me to see how these humans with their intelligence and understanding dealt with it. They had some sort of belief that physical death was not the end of a person, I knew that The Maker Of All Things had granted them a dual nature and that the spirit did actually live on but these people whose life was bound to the physical had to take on so much belief without actually seeing anything. And yet they seemed to know.

It came time for Sett and Tam to leave childhood behind and become men. They were given spears and knives and taken into the mountains by Ban who then came back alone. After two days Tam returned alone, carrying the leg of a deer and there was a celebration, he sat with the adults and they gathered round the fire and ate and drank and shared stories.

Sett's mother grew anxious until he came over the hill the next day dragging a frame made of wood with a young boar on it. The boar was still alive but tied securely. The next evening the boar was slain and put on a spit over the fire. The camp had never had boar before and as they feasted they danced and sang about the fire. If Tam was sullen before he was more so now. He came down to the lake and started throwing stones into it. The feelings of humans are complicated, for there was malice in the action. After a while he got bored, perhaps he was waiting for some sort of response from me until it became obvious he wasn't going to get one, after one last long throw he went back to the camp.

It was not long after their ascension to manhood that their parents took them away towards the east in search of mates and I never saw them again.

Perhaps I had got too close to these people, with them change happens so rapidly because their lives are so short. Har died the next winter and again I felt the loss. He was taken into the hills but because of the roughness of the weather it wasn't for some time that his bones were retrieved, some of them were missing though this didn't seem to bother anyone.

That summer Rab and Moonpool went with the hunters into the mountains, they were too young yet to go out alone so this was not a rite of passage. When they all returned they had a greater quantity of skins than ever before. Ban couldn't stop praising Moonpool for the accuracy of her arrows and the ease of catching deer and Rab for his strength and endurance, Lia hung on every word.

As the earth rolled slowly onwards through the seasons it seemed at times to roll too fast for me. It wasn't long before Rab and Moonpool in their turn were sent out alone and returned as adults. And still the seasons came and went. I could see Ban's hair begin to turn grey. As his time drew near he would often sit on the hill and wait.

"Moonpool." I heard his voice from the depths of the lake. "You have not appeared for a long time now."

What was there to say?

"Rab is growing into a man, he will lead the people and I was hoping ..."

Whenever I take on human form I get too involved, I yearn to be part of them but I do not want to forget who or what I am.

"If Rab is with me next time I come, will you ..."

I knew what he was asking but I also knew I needed to keep away. So I did.Father and son often went to the hill for some time and still I did not appear. Then, one night, a night of a full Moon, Ban and Rab came to the lake with fire on a large stone which they lay on the shore. Ban handed Rab a spear which Rab broke after a bit of effort and tossed it into the lake.

"Moonpool." Said Rab. "If I have offended you I am truly sorry."

Again I felt it best not to respond, for these people to develop as they should they do not need me to interfere. I hoped they would get on with their lives and rely less on me, but was part of my reluctance to appear my fear of so much change?

"You need to appear to them, this is part of their development." The Maker urged.

And that was all. He never explains, but it is best just to accept and obey.

I stood ankle deep in the lake. "You have not offended me."

Ban and his son knelt down on the shore.

"I told you before, Ban, this is not necessary."

"But it is." Said Ban. "I know why you do not come and I respect you for it. Bless my son now and I will not trouble you again."

"Rab." I said. "Stand on your feet and face me as a man."

Ban remained on his knees while Rab stood but it was hard for him to hold my gaze.

"You are to be leader and as humanity grows on this world you and your descendants will be remembered."

"I am not my father, I am still young."

"And I may be older than this world yet I am young too. We each of us do our best, we learn and grow."

"And I am growing old, Moonpool." Said Ban finally standing. "You have been good to us and I am grateful. I wish you well in the future, do not worry if you forget me for I am nothing in the order of the things, I pass as do all my kind. You are goddess and you are so much greater than me, I am glad we became, as much as is possible, friends."

And I was gone.

Chapter 7

Change

The hardest thing for me to bear in the years that followed was the death of Ban. The first human I ever met, the man who gave me my first understanding of humanity, was no more. He also was a part of the humanity that could be part of me when I let it. I do not understand what happens to the spark within the humans when their bodies die, their being is different from mine. But even without appearing in human form I was deeply saddened at his death.

The night after they took his body to the hills then Rab came and stood and gazed across the lake and this reminded me of the first time I had seen Ban, he looked so like him. There were tears in his eyes, but he stood straight and proud, he was his father's son. The sky was overcast and heavy, it would rain before long and a cold damp wind was already blowing up from the west. Rab shivered and drew his skins close round himself. He bowed his head then turned and slowly returned to the camp.

They brought Ban's bones back to the camp some days later and placed them in the first hut and lay dried grasses over them. Many people would come and talk to Ban and ask his blessing on the matters of the camp and their own personal hopes and fears.

Rab was a good leader and the group grew and did well under his leadership, and gradually people would come to him rather than his father's bones. He gained a mate from another group down the valley and they had many children together.

Rab's eldest son, Sten, was presented to me and in turn Sten presented his son, Hab. Hab presented Tal and Tal presented Thir. I would appear only for these occasions, this had become part of their ritual but beyond this I did not want to get so close to any human again.

Over the years I saw a side of humanity that was dark and at times wicked. Ban had once said "but some of them fear you and not all are peaceful." I didn't understand this at the time. Also the occasion when Tam threw stones into the lake had puzzled me. But many occasions I saw one person do well and another badly and I began to understand resentment and hatred. As Thir grew to be a man and Tal began to fade I saw that five of the other young men and three of the young women kept apart from the others.

One day Por, the tallest and obviously the leader of the smaller group stood in the centre of the camp, the others gathered behind him.

"Thir." He called. After a while he called again. "Thir!"

Thir emerged from the hut and stood alone facing Por. He said nothing.

"Who made you leader?"

"My father made me leader, and his father before him. Way back to Ban the Mighty."

"I know nothing of Ban. Who made your father leader?"

With that Tal emerged, still strong and straight but his hair was beginning to grey.

"Ban brought us here, he found this place and we settled here." Said Thir.

"I know nothing of Ban."

"His bones are here and his spirit watches over us. As does Moonpool, take care not to anger her."

"Moonpool, Moonpool, there is no such person, I see no Moonpool."

"We owe all to Moonpool, the fish in the lake, the deer on the hills, even the boar in the forests."

"Your only claim is that you were presented to someone who does not exist. The rest of us have not seen her. Look," He picked up a stone and threw it into the lake. "It is only a lake."

Perhaps I was wrong, I should have kept out of this, but I tossed it back and it landed at his feet.

No one spoke for a while.

"A trick." Said Por. He cast a wary glance at the lake.

"Be careful, Por, if you anger Moonpool we could all be in trouble."

"Ha. You cannot frighten me."

With that Por raised a thick piece of antler that had a rounded lump on the end and would have struck Thir, but Thir was quick and ducked the blow, wrestling Por to the ground, the antler rolling down the slope away from them.

Tal didn't move but watched the young men as they wrestled and punched. I wondered at this but it seems he trusted in his son's ability to prove himself. Only when one of the others following Por advanced on them did he raise the spear he had in his hand, aimed it at him and shook his head.

"This is between them."

The other backed down.

Soon Thir stood, panting and Por lay stunned and bleeding. The whole group that had followed Por began to move towards Thir, Tal glanced over at the lake with deep concern in his eyes, or maybe a mix of fear and pleading, they all had weapons and no one else in the camp was about.

Time to act, this I couldn't keep out of, so I appeared between Por and his followers, facing Por.

"Enough." I said. "Thir has proved himself a worthy leader. If you cannot follow him then form your own camp somewhere else."

I appeared much fiercer than I had ever done before; this surprised me as much as it frightened them. Por scrabbled backwards in his attempt to get up and get away from me at the same time. His followers all dropped their weapons and stepped backwards. No one ran but calmly if very nervously they moved away, gathered together some items necessary for a journey and began to move off eastwards without a word.

Tal and Thir sank to their knees before me. But before either of them spoke I was gone. I was gone to my thin place.

"O Maker Of All Things I am sorry, I have interfered, I have .."

"You could have done more but you didn't. You are a guardian and you did not overstep your position. You have nothing to be sorry for, you kept the peace. But be aware, every action has its repercussion and you will live through them and learn greater wisdom from them."

"Is someone going to get hurt because of me?"

"Someone is always hurt, that is the consequence of an imperfect world. You are not to blame because you do not know the future." And he said no more.

This worried me. The Maker Of All Things can be so obscure and I still felt I had made a mistake. There would be consequences and whether I understood or not I would be responsible.

Chapter 8

Reunion

The earth rolled on and on and season followed season. Eventually Por returned, but not to the camp. He, along with a much larger group than he had left with, five and five and two, climbed up beside Little Rainbow's waterfall on the south side. They climbed to the top of the hill and settled there, not the highest hill but the nearest to the lake. Already there was substantial woodland. The sun passed overhead many times before they had cleared a space on the hill and made three huts around the central fire.

Tal and Thir were standing, gazing across the lake, both in silence. They often stood there. They spoke very little but drew strength from each other in the calm. This day was calm and still, the Sun was high in the sky and a gentle breeze ruffled the surface of the lake.

This day they saw the smoke coming from the fire on the hill the other side of the lake.

"Do you see the smoke?" Asked Tal.

"Yes." Replied Thir "I wonder what that can be."

"There are people there surely, a new people. We should go and make ourselves known."

"I wonder if they know we are here?"

"They must have seen the smoke from our fire or the light from it in the night. In any case, we should go and find out who they are and what their intentions are."

"They are the other side of the lake so we shouldn't need to interfere with each other."

"Yes but they are still close. You and I will go, we shouldn't take a lot of people with us then they will know we come in peace."

"Very well. But how should we get there. It is a very long way round the lake to the west."

"We could go down the valley beyond the waterfall and back up that side, as long as we can find a way across the river."

"If only we could cross the lake in a boat but I fear Moonpool."

"I suppose the best way is offer her something and plead with her. After the business with Por we need to tread very carefully. But what sort of offering do you make to such a goddess? What is valuable to us may have no value to her."

"Perhaps just the act of giving her something will be enough."

In the end they knelt at the lakeside, tossed an antler knife in and asked my permission to cross the lake if they hollowed out a log to make a boat.

They were so unsure of me that I was unable to speak directly to either of them, so I spoke to Ness, their holy woman, in a dream, she was a very open woman and cared greatly for the people. I asked why they hadn't made a boat before as it would make fishing much easier and give them access to the other side of the lake, so of course they had my permission.

Sometimes I do find humans a bit narrow in their thought. They live in the valley without a problem but remain in awe of the lake, they didn't seem to realise I don't only dwell in the lake but I find people do have a strange sort of reverence for water everywhere. It is not their natural environment and they are right to be in awe of it, a sudden storm can be quite dangerous.

The next morning Ness told Thir of her dream. So he and Tal felled a reasonably sized tree and hollowed out a section of the trunk, they made two oars and the two men gingerly climbed into the boat and paddled across the lake. They had obviously done all this before because they knew exactly what they were doing but not here. By this time the other camp was complete and many of them, including Por, had gone away to hunt leaving only a few to tend the fire and guard the camp.

The journey across the lake was not a short one as they had to paddle round a headland and diagonally across the lake. They paddled into a secluded bay and pulled the boat onto the shore. From there it was only a short walk up the valley to Por's camp, although they had no idea at that time who had settled there.

"Heloo!" They called several times as they approached so they couldn't be accused of creeping up on them.

So when they arrived at the camp the five and three who had not gone with the hunters were waiting, they had spears in their hands but not in a threatening way, rather with the end resting on the ground. On the other hand Tal and Thir had only a sharp piece of antler between them tucked into Tal's belt.

"Tal, Thir, it is you." Said one of the women.

"Stell." Said Tal in disbelief and surprise. "You're back, but why here, why not to the camp? Is Por with you?"

"Por is away hunting. This is his camp, he is in charge here."

"Then why come back at all?"

"Come into the camp, sit by the fire, have something to eat I will tell you."

During the meal Stell told them of their travels, the suspicion they often met with as a band looking for somewhere to settle that they never had as traders, she spoke of empty lands but they were empty for a reason and there was no way they could settle there.

"Por didn't want to join another clan because Moonpool had told him to start his own camp and all the good land seems to have been settled. He then decided that it would be a good idea to settle near this lake, there is plenty of space, the land is good and the hunting is plentiful. Por was quite reluctant to come back at first but there really was no other option. When we got here we saw nothing of Moonpool herself even though we waited a while at the top of the waterfall so reasoned she wasn't going to object."

"No she hasn't objected, in fact it was her who encouraged us to come and make ourselves known so it must be alright. I only wish she had told Ness who you were, we had no idea. I am glad to see you back and I hope we can put the past behind us." Said Tal.

"When is Por coming back?" Thir asked. He seemed a little on edge.

"We don't know. They only left yesterday so it could be a few days yet. " Admitted Stell.

"Tell him we came, he knows where we are and he will always be welcome. Yes, there is plenty of space and we hope you do well here."

He stood and turned to go. Then he turned back. "I am glad you have all returned. There is much I have regretted."

Tal and Thir returned to their camp and told them the news, there were mixed feeling about this but generally people were glad. They had been through much together and they were family. It would be a chance to put things right.

Many days later Por and the hunters returned and learned of their visit. Por was silent. He went to the top of Little Rainbow's waterfall and sat looking down at the cascading water and listened to Little Rainbow laughing and singing. He sat for ages in silence before returning to the camp.

Shortly after this I went and sat with Little Rainbow, both of us in human form though we hadn't planned to do this. Little Rainbow was small and fair and bright, her hair silver and sparkling, her eyes green and full of mystery and her thin dress could almost be a rainbow itself.

"What do you think of Por?" She asked.

"Por was frustrated last time I saw him, in many ways he would have made a better leader than Thir but that was not up to me. I am glad he has come back to set up his own camp and hopefully they are far enough from each other for them both to live in peace and close enough to heal the rift. "

"That would be a good thing, from what I hear that is not always the case with humans. Especially when there is an argument over land and the land is not theirs anyway."

"It is not always the case with us either though I have never understood what we have to argue about anyway."

She laughed.

"You are old, beyond the age of this world." She began and then paused before continuing. "You know many things and have understanding from beyond."

There was silence for a while. This didn't bother me as I still had little conception of the passing of time. But it seemed to bother her, her life began with the waterfall and she was very young. I looked at her, I had never known her so serious, I began to be a little suspicious. I was aware that Por had sat here, and his band would have been the first humans Little Rainbow had seen close up.

"This is a dangerous form for us to take." I said. "I don't take it often. We have feelings because of having a heart and blood that even I do not understand. Don't give in to feelings."

"Is that why you hid from Ban?"

"I thought you were supposed to be the young one, Little Rainbow." This did cut me to my human heart and I could still feel the loss deeply in this form. "How wise and perceptive you are. But, I repeat, it is dangerous for us to feel. Ban was wise enough to see this and in a way wiser than me."

"Tâf brings me news. Some of our kind have taken on human form and have mixed with the humans, some even have borne children."

"And all have either aged and died or returned and had to exist with greater loss. I may not have borne you but in many ways I am mother to you, or grandmother or whatever. Take my advice. Do not get too close to Por, you have not had much experience with humans yet and he is the first you have met. He is a good man but he is a man and you are a sprite. You were made for dancing, light and joy, humans have to suffer an awful lot."

Somehow I felt what I said had fallen on deaf ears and I feared for the future.

The Earth rolled on and on for many more days before Por and Stell made their own boat and paddled over to Ban's camp. Thir welcomed them with open arms, all anxiety gone. They were reunited to many old friends and family. They were given such a feast as rarely happened on days when the Sun or the Moon were not at important places in the sky. My heart would have been glad if I had been in human form at the time, especially when I saw how Por and Stell were together, particularly as I knew Stell was bearing a son. I did wonder if Little Rainbow knew this.

The fire was built right up and there was dancing and beating of branches on logs and there was singing. There was also drinking out of the special skins that had fermented honey, something Thir's brother Thane had brought back from his last trading trip. Such was the relief and the joy that I was tempted to join them but I was glad enough just to watch.

When eventually sleep took over they slept well past the dawn and some almost to midday. Many of them were rough and when they appealed to Ness for something for a strange ailment they were given no sympathy, she knew what it was having spent years over the hills to the west learning about healing and herbs among other things.

Later that day Por and Stell took their leave having renewed many friendships and got re-acquainted with family. As they got into the boat many of the folk placed gifts of food and beads into the boat, and Thane told Por where to trade for the special skins.

It was a bright sunny day and the gentle breeze hardly rippled the surface of the lake. As they paddled back Stell paused and let her hand skim over the surface of the lake.

"I am with child?" I heard her thought clearly.

"You are. This is an important child, it is his first, call me if you need me. But tell me this; why is Por not angry with me?"

"You are goddess, why would he be angry with the lake or the hills or the Moon?"

Por paused also and turned to see why she had stopped paddling and seeing the look in her eyes he smiled, he reached out his hand and grasped hers for a moment. Then they took up their paddles again.

I detected a lot of Ban in Por, he may not have been eldest son of eldest son through the generations but he was still of Ban's blood. He was descended from Ban's daughter Moonpool and had a lot of her strength and independence too. Although he did not have the depth of wisdom of Ban he would still have made a good leader for the people, but it was not my place to decide that for them. Besides, the valley is large and the people need to spread out into it, there would inevitably be other camps in the valley and this had started well. If this was the consequence of my action then I was glad.

When it was Stell's time I sat with her and Fan, the holy woman of Por's settlement, and to my surprise so did Little Rainbow. She was very wistful and I could see she was wrestling with many different emotions. I was glad she was here as this was an experience she needed for many reasons.

"This child is truly blessed," Said Fan not in the least surprised. "That both of you are here."

"Moonpool is the expert here." Said Little Rainbow. "This is all new to me I have come to learn as much as to help."

I let her hold Stell's hand and channel peace and strength, and to take some of the pain. I hoped she would learn something of the pain and anguish that is part of the human lot but that it wouldn't detract from her joy and laughter as a sprite.

Stell also had Ban's blood in her and she was strong, the birth was relatively easy if you can call any human birth easy. Even so I knew that this was quite a shock for Little Rainbow, until the birth which was a wonder to her. The son of Por was born safe and well and cried out and I made sure we were gone before Por entered the hut.

Por took his son out and presented him to the world. "This is Uban, son of Por."

Chapter 9

Devastation

Por would often walk down the valley to the lake and gaze across, usually he came early in the morning so where he stood was in the shade and the morning sun was shining on the far shore. I thought he looked across somewhat wistfully towards the other camp. He was not an open man so I had no idea what he thought, did he regret leaving or did he resent that he hadn't gained supremacy. But he had made his decision and he had his responsibilities, he seemed happy with his group and he was delighted with his family. He had also made his peace with Thir and surely he must have reasoned that he had made his peace with me also. Although he never spoke to me he did on one occasion toss an antler knife into the lake and bowed his head for a moment, then with a look of peace on his face he turned and returned to his family.

Uban grew to be a strong and agile man, a good hunter though not as astute as Por. He had his father's younger brashness as well as his looks. Por would send him back down the valley with any trading party because he was a very astute dealer and I suspected he was a little wary of the rivalry between them and didn't want to leave him in charge of the camp. After many cycles of the seasons Por took him to the top of the waterfall where Little Rainbow danced and sang as one with the water. They stood for a while and looked back at the lake which was calm and the slow drifting clouds in the blue sky were reflected in its still surface. Then they turned and looked down at the waterfall and watched the water dancing and singing and throwing out little rainbows transfixed for a while.

Por straightened up and called out, "Moonpool, Little Rainbow, behold Uban, my son and son of Ban, he will be chief after my day."

Little Rainbow took human form a little too eagerly I thought, so I felt I had better follow suit. Uban was a little startled as to him we were probably just tales. I was rather surprised that Por knew Little Rainbow to be calling her by name and I realised that I must have missed something in the times he would sit there for I wasn't aware they had actually met. I cannot be everywhere at once and when I knew he and Stell were together I saw no need to watch. Uban and Little Rainbow exchanged looks that I felt ominous. I had seen this look between humans and knew what it meant. I took hold of Little Rainbow's hand and tried to convey my concern without words, I couldn't speak of my concerns out loud. I couldn't speak to her in spirit either, because Little Rainbow had closed herself to me and I knew this was dangerous. Although this was the first time Uban had seen her yet the human heart is easily swayed by our natural beauty and Little Rainbow had ample time to watch Uban.

In my thin place I spoke to Light of the Long Hand for although I felt a sort of motherly responsibility to her she was a sprite not just of water but of light as well and as such reflected his light rather than Silverwheel's.

"Light, I fear for Little Rainbow, I fear she has feelings for Uban and he for her."

"I have seen this too. Little Rainbow is a sprite and very young, she is not as wise or as careful as you and Uban does not have Ban's wisdom. She will not talk to me or to Rainbow, she has set her heart on mortality and yet it is not her I fear for it is you."

"Me? Why?"

"She is only the sprite of the waterfall and as such she does not guard the lives of people nor ever will. In the days to come, if this is unstoppable, remember you are more than just a lake and you have already proved yourself over and over."

"I do not understand. I know I am more than just the lake but what do you mean?"

"I hope I am wrong. Thir has a sister, Ellan, as you know she is away in training at the moment but will be back soon, she will be the next holy woman, talk to her if anything bad happens."

"But, Little Rainbow, what should I do?"

"We can do nothing she has closed herself to us, we do not know the future, we cannot direct the lives of the humans and the lesser spirits are notoriously headstrong."

I stood at the head of the waterfall in physical form because she would not answer in spirit and called to Little Rainbow. Reluctantly she came. She was no longer full of joy and laughter and a sad and wistful change had come over her. The waterfall also seemed dark and flat, the water just dripping down as the rain on a stormy day despite the sun shining brightly overhead.

"You are not my mother, not in the sense humans have mothers." She said quite sharply.

"No, I am not but I do have a lot more experience."

"Experience? You hide from experience and you do not allow yourself to feel."

"And you take on human form too often. You forget what you are."

"I am a sprite, I am not important, my existence is frivolous."

"Oh Little Rainbow, you are spirit and earth and water and light, you are not frivolous you are joy and this world is in need of joy and quite possibly in the ages to come the need for joy will be greater. Humans are animals with intelligence and although they are also spirit their lives are short, they come and go."

"You still have feelings for Ban, I know this, and while you keep that in your heart he still is."

"I will always keep you in my heart as well if you do what you intend but the part of you in my heart will not be you any more than the part of Ban in my heart is Ban. I see the shadow of Ban in some of his descendants, like Por, but they are not him either, he is long gone and I remain."

I could see that this sank in, she had not thought of mortality.

"And this makes you sad." She said after a while the sharpness gone from her tone.

"Yes, it makes me sad, even when I am not in this form. Ban was the first human I ever met and I will admit I still do not understand my feelings. And, yes, I hide from them by not taking this form often but there are other reasons why I do not take this form often for I have possibly interfered too much already. Yet in this form I find I have such love for you and I regret not talking to you more often."

"I love you too and I can see so much sadness in you. I do not want always to be sad. I was not made to be sad."

"No, but you were made to be eternal."

"And what of the humans?"

"The Maker Of All Things has a secret about the humans after death that we do not know. Does he have this for us? None of us know, we were not meant to die."

She stood and thought for a long time, she was born with the waterfall and knew nothing of the vastness of the passing of ages. In a sense she was closer to the mortals than I was because of the shortness of her life so far so could I really blame her for feeling as she did. With no experience of a distant past perhaps she could not imagine a distant future, for her now was all there was.

She hugged me, it was like a goodbye, and then she was one with the waterfall again and for a while the waterfall danced in the sunlight but the little rainbows seemed dim.

After this she no longer listened and in no time at all she was in the camp with Uban. She stood before him and declared.

"I call Light of the Long Hand, Silverwheel and The Maker Of All Things as witness. I relinquish who I was and become who I am. Uban, take me."

As he took her, at the height of passion, several things happened. I saw a light go out of Little Rainbow, clouds rolled across the sky and a violent storm blew in from the west. The ground began to shake and my waters were whipped up and smashed against the head of the waterfall. Was this me? To this day I am still not sure. The land was torn apart and the waters flooded into the valley below. Too late I realised that the lake was gushing away and I was powerless to stop it.

The people in both camps were cowering in terror. Uban and Little Rainbow fell apart panting, she was sobbing.

"What have I done? What have I done?" She cried.

Uban was useless, he cowered in the back of the hut when he should have comforted her and reassured her, he was her man now and he was no man. And I was useless too.

The waters continued to flow away, exposing the ground. There was so much water in the lake this seemed to go on and on, even for someone who still had little perception of time. Then all was still. The water settled to a river that all the sodden ground continued to drain into for many days. The clouds rolled away and the Sun came out. My thin place was now exposed and I sat there in the mud unable to think or reason for many days.

Silverwheel and Light of the Long Hand sat with me. I had not seen them in human form before, Silverwheel glowing silvery blue and mysterious, Light of the Long Hand bright and golden and strong. The three of us were sitting in the mud.

"I am no longer Moonpool." I said eventually.

"You are always Moonpool." Said a voice that was neither Silverwheel nor Light of the Long Hand, but my eyes were too full of tears to see who it was.

I tried to focus on a figure before me, it seemed to be kneeling in the mud but I could not see clearly enough.

"This is your place and we will keep it as holy ground for all of time."

Slowly my eyes focussed, Silverwheel and Light of the Long Hand had gone and kneeling before me was Ness.

"But why has this happened? Are you angry with us?" She asked, shaking.

"I am not angry with you and I am not sure why this has happened. I only know that the sprite that had been the waterfall has taken on human form permanently and relinquished her spiritual self. Therefore there can no longer be a waterfall."

"But have you taken on human form permanently? Is that why you are sitting here in the mud? Is that why the lake has gone?"

I thought for a while, what am I without the lake? I have always been more than the lake, I am the whole valley. But how can I be Moonpool? Moonpool was the name Ban gave me because he saw the Moon reflected in the lake and recognised me as being one with that image and now the lake is gone and the Moon's reflection with it.

"I have only taken on this form for a while to think and to feel, I cannot feel as much otherwise." I drew my knees up to my chest and hugged them close, I felt so empty.

"And what of the waterfall, who is she now and where is she."

"Little Rainbow!" I cried out jumping up. In my own anguish I had forgotten her, her anguish must me much greater. Uban had not been there for her and neither had I.

In an instant I was with her. Stell was with her in the hut teaching her what it was to be a human woman, brushing her silver hair and singing gently to her. She seemed so young and sad and vulnerable. She was dressed in animal skins now and this seemed so wrong.

"Little Rainbow." I said, clasping her hands in mine, kneeling before her. "I am so sorry I left you."

"Oh Moonpool." She said close to tears, leaning forward so our heads came together. "I didn't know that without the waterfall there would be no lake, what have I done to you? I thought you had been washed away with the water."

Stell sat quietly back.

"I never was just the lake. But I am just not sure I am Moonpool anymore."

"And how can I be Little Rainbow?"

"You are human now and humans do find reasons for joy, not least in having children."

"But is that even possible?"

"Possible?" I sat back onto my heels and looked her full in the face. "In human form we are very fertile since we are nature spirits. With you it only took the one time and you have conceived."

Little Rainbow was startled, I released her hands. She looked down at herself and felt her stomach, then looked back up at me with wonder in her eyes.

"How can you know?" Asked Stell. "It is only a few days."

I smiled and Stell blushed, no explanation was needed.

"You need to tell Uban, he may yet prove himself." I said to her.

Stell looked down at the ground. "Uban has gone."

"He is not far, in fact he is returning with at least some determination. Little Rainbow, do you really love him?"

"Yes, yes I do. But how can I be Little Rainbow?"

There was now a glow about her, for these two pieces of news had brought back something of the sprite to her. She would never be a sprite but this would always be who she is. I looked at Stell and she looked at me, we nodded and smiled.

"There, I can still see Little Rainbow in you. You are still in my valley and I will still watch over you."

Little Rainbow gazed up at me and the love we felt for each other was like the warmth of the sun after a storm.

"Your valley, you have always been more than the lake and I can see that you are still Moonpool." Little Rainbow said in a quiet voice, a small smile on her lips.

Yes, my valley. Moonpool is who I am, lake or no lake.

"Stell." I said to her. "You are Little Rainbow's mother now and you are wise. I trust you to watch over her, this is all new to her and she needs you more than me."

"Thank you Moonpool. I am glad I have seen you again like this, you were rather scary last time." She smiled. "She is my daughter and I will care for her. Though how do you care for a goddess even when she has become mortal?"

"She is not a goddess, she was and still is to some extent a sprite and sprites are a little wayward. I do not understand everything that has happened to her. Perhaps she never will be completely human and because of that your family will receive blessing but treat her as human."

Chapter 10

Transformation

Uban returned, he was a man now and he had learned important lessons. He went to Little Rainbow and loved her deeply. He would often come down the valley to where the lake had been. He saw the mud that was left and the rivulets still draining down into the river. He would stand and gaze and sigh, what had been done could not be undone now. He felt strongly that he had caused this and kept apologising to me. To begin with the clouds kept up a steady drizzle, then after a few days the clouds rolled away and the Sun came out and began to dry the land. This then was the consequence of my action so if it was anyone's fault it was mine.

"Uban." I said gently in his mind. "We are all at fault or none of us. To feel is human and it is spirit too. None of us can foresee the consequences of our actions but as we live we learn and we grow."

"But you are goddess."

"I feel and make mistakes and learn too, I am far older than you but I hope I will never be too old to learn. Sometimes I feel it is only since you all came and settled here that I have really begun to learn at all."

"This is still my fault."

"There is no fault, this is life and life goes on and adjusts. There is no lake between you and Thir now, perhaps this was meant to be."

Little Rainbow had a son without any trouble, human she may have been but she was also nature and nature is life and fruitfulness. Uban presented his son Carn to the camp and Ban's camp were invited to join the celebrations. In fact there was a lot of coming and going between the two camps, a lot of sharing, once the river settled down and they found a fairly shallow part to wade across and the land had become dry enough.

Trade to the east had become easier as they built boats which they could paddle down the river from the centre of the valley past several settlements, some of which were rebuilding after the flood which fortunately hadn't killed anyone, and all the way to the port by the sea. Carn, when he was old enough was sent over the hills to the west to learn the ways of wisdom and healing, because of his mother he had what the humans called a natural magic and he was destined to become a great holy man who people from all over would come to consult. As were his son and his son and so through the generations. This left his younger brother, Con, to lead the camp, and his sons after him and although he was a little wayward because of who his mother was he was a good leader and after Uban's death she was still well able to keep him in check.

The land dried and grass and trees and shrubs grew readily on the rich soil. Ness made sure that the low mound that was my thin place was kept clear of all but lush grass. Every important phase of the Moon and every significant position of the sun she led a ceremony here. She even, with my permission, brought Ban's bones, or what was left of them after such a long time, and buried them at the point nearest the rising Sun of the equinox.

Ban's camp moved down into the valley a little distance from the mound. Unfortunately the river was prone to flooding and the camp had to be abandoned and built again further up. At times like this I realised how much I missed the lake. The strange thing was that although the river flooded and the waters were higher than the mound the flow of water meant that the mound was never again submerged. And there were times in the fading of each year when a mist filled the valley and reminded me of the lake.

The lack of a lake to hide in was strangely liberating. When I was not in human form I didn't just retreat to my thin place but rode the wind and lay in the soil and grew with the trees and sang with the birds. I was more aware of all the living things in the valley and even felt closer to the two camps.

So when Little Rainbow neared the end, having seen her children to five generations, I was immediately aware and sat with her and held her close. I wondered than no one else was there but I have noticed with humans that when an elder has been around for a long time they irrationally believe that they will live for ever but this was so especially in Little Rainbow's case because they knew she was a sprite.

"Moonpool, I am scared, what will happen to me?"

I so wanted her to be in my thin place that I found that we were. It happened that it was the equinox and the Sun was sinking in the west. I sat on the grass and cradled her close.

"You will surely have your answer here." I said to her. Then I lifted up my head to the sky. "O Maker Of All Things please can you give Little Rainbow a sign."

She looked up to the Sun, her face glowed in the light, and she smiled. A mist was settling in the valley and a little rainbow glowed about her head. I smoothed her hair still silver and thick.

"There, Little Rainbow, you have your answer, the future is not dark and you are safe to go."

I felt as if my heart was almost torn from my body as she let out her last breath as a slow sigh and died in peace. In spirit I saw her leave her body, young and joyful as she was when I first knew her, laughing and dancing. And she was gone beyond where I could see.

I sat for ages cradling her lifeless body until several members of her family arrived somewhat perplexed, and on seeing her bursting into tears. I let her go into their arms and they held her and wept.

"Bury her here with Ban's bones." I said. "This is not a place of death but of life."

Then the Sun sank behind the hills, the end of a day.

Chapter 11

Circle

The Earth rolled on and on, the seasons came and went. Many generations passed, I could list them all but you would not want to read that list. The line in both camps went from father to eldest son if there was one, sometimes to daughter and sometimes there were no children so it went to brother's child. When there were many children the second child was sent over the hill to the east to the Oak Thicket to learn the ways of wisdom and holiness.

Ban's camp was now five huts, the most recent two had walls made of stones. Por's camp had become Pole's camp over the ages because of mishearing in one instance. But it remained the same size as many of the offspring went east in search of more excitement.

It was a night of the full Moon when a man came to my thin place and just stood. He just stood gazing. I could not understand why he just stood there, was he waiting for something or was something going on in his inner being? But I realised I was waiting too, and I knew I had done this before and there was something about him that reminded me of Ban.

This man wore cloth weaved of plants and he had no weapons at all. I stood behind him and waited. I smelt the earth, and the growing plants and felt the grass under my feet. There was no breeze and the surface of the river rippled over the stones in the river bed and the Moon was reflected in the water and wavered and splintered with the flowing river. I could hear the slow steady breathing of the man and the strong beat of his mortal heart.

He drew in a breath and let it out slowly. He uttered the sound of the first word I had ever heard, "Moonpool."

"Moonpool." I repeated and something stirred in my heart.

He gave a start but did not run. I have seen so many creatures run after such a start, sensing danger. But in his surprise he must have reasoned there was no danger because he knew of me and possibly was hoping to see me. Slowly he turned and saw me. He gazed at me for some time, turned back to look at the river and turned back to me again.

"Moonpool?" He said to me with a questioning look in his eye.

"Colban." I said in reply. "You have returned a wise man."

Colban was the brother of Tharon the present leader of Ban's camp. He had been sent to the Oak Thicket as a boy. I am not permitted to enter there but I could tell from Colban he had done very well, he was a very open person and allowed me to see deep into his soul. Besides, not only did he have the oak staff but he was also wearing the oak crown and this was awarded very rarely.

He was about to get down on his knees.

"No, don't do that."

But he did anyway.

"I am a mortal man and you are a goddess, it is only right. And besides I am intruding in your sacred space."

"No you are not intruding. This place is as much yours and all the peoples as it is mine. Now stand on your feet."

He remained on his knees.

"With your permission." He actually looked up at me at this point. "I would like to have a ditch dug and a bank made to mark your holy place. Such is the custom in many places now, though here the ditch should be outside the bank because of the river, it will make this more of an island when the river floods."

"That would be good."

"I have observed the shape of the place and it is very interesting, it is an almost perfect ellipse. And if we make it more obviously an ellipse it will naturally align with the sun at both equinoxes."

"And what are you gaining from this?"

"I understand that Ban and Little Rainbow are buried here."

Both deaths still hurt and I couldn't hide this from him. "They are."

"This holy place is central to the lives of both communities, if I am to guide them in spiritual matters I need your blessing and I need their attachment to their beginnings."

"Both communities? What of Calmar?"

"I will not hide from you and I beg your pardon, he has the blood of Little Rainbow and I do not, but I feel I am better equipped than he is."

"He is older than you as well. So this is a power thing then." I said sounding perhaps a little harsher than I meant. But I did need to be sure of his intentions for this might not go well with Calmar. “It is such a struggle for you humans because you do not always know your place.”

He looked up a little startled but saw the smile on my face and because of his openness we were able to share much that was unsaid.

“Because of Little Rainbow perhaps I have been a little lenient with her descendants from time to time.” I said in a softer voice. “You are right however, and her line is weakened by time whereas I see Ban’s strength in you reborn. Such is the way with humans. Colban, will you stand at last or I cannot give my blessing.”

He stood and faced me though he was a little shorter than me.

“There now.” I said. “To see eye to eye that is blessing enough. Dig the ditch and build the bank, make this an important place for the people.”

He bowed his head in reverence.

“However, I ask again. What of Calmar?” I asked.

“You know Calmar better than I.”

“Calmar has been a good and faithful holy man for a long time and he is not going to like this. I have seen the rivalry between humans and with it the resentment.”

“The teaching we have both received speaks against such rivalry. We are all equal.”

“What have you learned of human nature? I fear Calmar has not leaned this, he has never once sought me because he fears my power and resents my authority. You have the oak crown and therefore he will see you as greater than himself and he will resent you for it no matter how much you try to treat him as an equal.”

"He did receive an oak staff did he not? He did complete his training. He should not feel this way."

"I hope you are right. Well, dig the ditch and build the bank but do so together with Calmar and seek his advice, he does have age and experience on his side."

And then I left him to save the embarrassment of him walking away from me.

Chapter 12

Dissention

Calmar was put out. He would come to the river opposite my thin place and glare across, he was not an open person in his thoughts but I could read bitterness in every fibre of his being as he stood there. He would come in the evening just as the Sun went down because he knew Colban came in the morning. Often he would stand in the pouring rain and grind his teeth as this suited his mood. Mortals can be very strange at times. I could see no purpose in this. He was avoiding coming at the same time as Colban so who was this aimed at? Was it me in particular or to the spirits in general or even The Maker Of All Things at the unfairness of life? Humans almost never blame themselves for their own failings.

Perhaps I should have said but it was not my place to do so but he hadn't actually finished his training since he couldn't remember everything he was taught, at least he had been there and had been trained and he should have known how to behave. He had been the only resident holy man in the two communities for many years and since he had held the post when no one else could he thought he was indispensable. So when Colban suddenly appeared with the oak crown only given to one student every five years he felt threatened. And when Colban proclaimed he had a vision of Moonpool and in honour of her was going to make her holy place a proper temple for all the people, he became very sullen. Colban did consult him on this and tried to get him involved, deferring to him as knowing the people better.

"Calmar." Colban pleaded with him. "You know the people, you have led them in celebration in Moonpool's holy place for many years and if we are to do this thing for her we both need to be involved. It will also honour Ban and Little Rainbow as a fitting memorial to both of them. This is a good thing for many reasons, surely you can see this."

"I do not see the need. You are asking everyone to put aside some of their other work for something they probably won't want. We have done very well over the years, everyone knows where the holy place is and that Ban and Little Rainbow are both there."

"Yes, they do now. But after such a long time the knowledge is like a vague story and in time it may fade altogether. We need to mark this special site that future generations will not forget. Do people still go there to talk to Ban or Little Rainbow? Do they talk to Moonpool?"

Calmar knew they didn't and that even he never consulted me but he could not admit to this.

"At least ask them if they would be willing for this." Said Colban seeing Calmar was silent and guessing the reason.

"Very well, I will ask."

Both communities were enthusiastic about Colban's plan and set to work with antler hooks to loosen the earth and wooden spades to dig the ditch and pile the earth at my thin place. Calmar was now also angry at the people for falling in with Colban and ignoring his advice. He would come among them when they were tired and ask why there was need for this.

"This place has stood here from the beginning of time, Ban is buried here and my distant mother Little Rainbow, is Colban saying it is not good enough?" He asked.

"Colban had a vision and he has the oak crown, if Moonpool wants this it must be right." Tharon, leader of Ban's camp replied.

"No one has seen Moonpool, ever, not as far as anyone remembers, so how do we know that she wants this. We only have his word that it is what Moonpool wants. It is what he wants not Moonpool at all."

"I have seen her for I was presented to her by my father." Stated Tharon. "I'm sure she will be pleased with this."

"I have seen her too when my father presented me to her." Affirmed Ralton of camp Pole. "Come on Calmar you have been a good holy man and we are grateful for all that you have done but you don't know everything."

"And Colban does?"

"He has the oak crown."

"And how can you say no one has ever seen her?" Asked Tharon. "You are a holy man so surely you speak to her often."

This conversation stung Calmar as he had no answer. It was not meant with any spite but so often humans feel such things when none is intended because their own hearts are dark. He didn't stay after this but strode back to his camp.

In the night he would mutter to anyone who would listen in camp Pole.

"I am Little Rainbow's heir, are you going to stand for this? We are her people, not Moonpool's."

I do not like to interfere and this was something they had to work through themselves. So I waited and watched.

"Moonpool has been good to us." Said Tarel sleepily.

"But who do you think will have precedence in the new temple?" He asked. "Camp Ban or Camp Pole?"

"We do so much together; we have always celebrated the solstice there together under your guidance. Why should it be different now?"

"Colban, he is not interested in us, he lives down there and they are nearer to the temple."

"He lives down there because you live up here and he doesn't want to intrude. It is because you think he will take over from you but he doesn't seem to be like that. He seems to be a very humble man and insists you are equals. Surely you can work together."

"Do you really think we won't have much say in this new temple?" Asked Sarak.

"Oh go to sleep, don't listen to him Sarak, I'm tired and I am not interested." Said Tarel. "Calmar you're only put out because you didn't have the oak crown. Come to think of it you didn't have the oak staff either, the one you use you made yourself." Finishing in a mumble Tarel fell asleep.

This passing remark stung again. Calmar had always resented the lack of formal acceptance by those at the oak thicket and had hoped that no one here would know, for all these years no one had questioned his right to be a holy man, not until now. Not until they had seen

Colban with the oak crown and the oak staff that was so different to Calmar's.

"You can see what Colban is doing can't you Sarak. He is setting us against each other. He comes among us with his humble words but flaunts his staff and his crown for everyone to know we are not equals."

"Tarel does have a point though."

"Maybe, but you mark my words. Colban will not care for us up here. For all his smooth words and kindly demeanour it is show only. For years now the two camps have worked together and he wishes to divide us. He is even dividing us in this camp against each other."

"For whatever reason Colban doesn't come here and we do have you."

"Yes, you can be assured that I will never let you down."

I had come across many like Calmar before. They would always find someone who would listen and people who listened were like them, you always got discord somewhere. I was not going to interfere this time. They would have to make their own minds up so I left them alone.

The next day there were a few missing at the dig from Camp Pole, this included Calmar and Sarak. It was time for Colban to try and ease tensions, to try and get close to Calmar, so he went up with those from the camp in the evening. He was welcomed warmly into the camp by most of them and shared food. He sat by Calmar and talked to him normally. He stayed as they settled in for the night.

"What are you trying to do?" Asked Calmar.

"What was the overriding lesson we were taught?"

Calmar said nothing.

"Our role is to serve, to heal, to teach, to advise and to be a bridge to the gods."

"So?"

"The greatest lesson is that you and I are equal and there is not one greater than the other. The crown is to encourage us to be the best we can possibly be and not for ourselves but in the service of others. I do need your help and experience. Although there are many family relationships this is still two camps and we must be one or there will be bloodshed. If we have a hard winter and food is scarce you and I need to keep the peace."

"Equal? No such thing. You have your oak crown and your plans for the hump by the river. I know what you are after. You believe you are so much better than I am and you want to rule all the people. You have visions from Moonpool so who can argue? As for bloodshed, that will not come from me."

"You are wrong, I seek peace." Colban leant back. "But I see you will never believe me. I will not summon Moonpool this is beneath her. You and I must sort this out between us and that will take time. Come to the river tomorrow and see."

The next day all the people came together to finish the work. The ditch and the bank were soon finished. Calmar stood at a distance, at least he came.

Colban stood at the east end just in front of where Ban and Little Rainbow were buried facing the people with the setting equinox sun on his face.

"Gather round." He called.

All the people put down their tools and gathered in the enclosure facing him.

"Brother Calmar, stand with me if you will."

Calmar was not going to move, this was not an order it was a request but he was just not going to comply. For the sake of peace I took his arm, such was his surprise he let me lead him through the people who parted for us as surprised as he was, after all I had practically faded into legend and many were unsure of my existence including Calmar. So I took him to stand with Colban and was about to not be there.

"Moonpool." Was that a plea in Colban's eye? "Now we are all here will you bless your temple and us your servants?"

I smiled at him and took up a position on the bank behind them both, placing my hands on their heads. There are times when we may give the effect of wings as the higher beings have. And because of Colban's unwavering belief in me now was a time when it was possible. So this I did though mine are more like the wings of a butterfly than of a bird, I would never presume, they were very large and dark though somewhat transparent and the setting sun glinted on them and I spread them over those closest to me.

"You are all children of Ban, Ban the good, Ban the wise. I thank you for your work here and although here you may talk to me remember I am only a servant of The Maker Of All Things and in His Name I bless Colban, Calmar, this place and all of you."

Chapter 13

Unease

Calmar was still not happy, but what could he do. Colban saw them as equals but he did not, his nature would not let him. In his mind someone had to be the head priest and someone the assistant, meaning him. My presence had put him in an awkward position in that I had blessed them both in the eyes of everyone, but he knew my right hand had been on Colban and my left on him. Even I could not have persuaded him I did not have a superior hand because I do not really have hands at all. For him it was symbolic anyway and he felt the sting of it deeply because no one else could possibly see it his way, they all saw me bless them both equally. So he could only bide his time.

Still he kept coming to the river opposite the temple and he would stand and glare across in the fading light of the setting Sun and even that could not brighten his mood, it might just as well be raining as he carried his own cloud around with him. His fists clenched and his closed mind plotting. My appearance hadn't helped him at all. Now he had someone definite to be angry with. Before he had just felt cheated by fate because he didn't really believe in anything beyond what he could see, and he now knew there were spirits and if anything this made him feel smaller.

The temple became more than just a place to gather for significant times of the year. It became the place for a ceremony when a person died, for when two people came together and asked for a blessing that they might have children and a place to bring each new child to give thanks. Calmar and Colban would perform the rite for their own camps. When a person died this involved bringing the body to the site at sunset, placing it at the western end with little gifts from the people, an invocation from the priest and the blessing with blood and water. Then the body is taken outside the temple and placed on a pile of wood and burned and when all is burned the ashes are scattered on the river.

The problem being that the folk of Camp Pole would rather Colban took all the ceremonies as they were not sure Calmar was really genuine. They could not help but draw comparisons because as both camps were so interrelated most people attended the funerals of both camps. Colban was approached with requests on the basis that the person was born in camp Ban or was related in some way to someone who was. But Colban would not.

The problem was worse when two people came together and they were from different camps so Colban would insist that the holy man from the camp of the woman would always preside.

Calmar was bitter then for two reasons, one that his own people rejected him and two that Colban was being condescending, which he was not. So intent was he that he was being slighted in every way there was now no way through to him.

The winter solstice came and in the night the two holy men led their people with fire in bowls of fired clay, something I had not seen before but knew that people away east had learned the art of firing clay. They placed their bowls on a stone slab that had been brought down from the mountains especially for the occasion by many men and placed on smaller upright stones at the eastern end of the temple.

Calmar went round to the other side of the stone and Colban stood between the stone and the people, both facing east, waiting for the rising sun. They raised their arms in unison and began to chant, Colban's voice rich and deep, Calmar's thin and cracked. All the people joined in as one. The sound resonated in the heart of the valley and carried down the river.

A gust of wind blew up the valley and Calmar's fire flickered and went out, this was not my doing. He did not see this as his back was to the stone and his face was to the east. Colban quietly and carefully tipped some of the fire from his bowl into the other so Calmar wouldn't know. Unfortunately everyone else saw this.

As the sky brightened in the east the people's voices grew louder until there was a shout from every throat as the Sun broke above the hill. Then there was celebration, feasting and drinking, a new year had begun, the Sun had returned.

In the days that followed there was talk, Calmar's fire had gone out therefore he did not speak for the gods. I hoped Calmar wouldn't hear about this but he did and I was the obvious spirit to blame. Colban did ask me about this and I assured him it had not been me, but there are other spirits and one of them must have had a reason unless it was purely chance.

No one outwardly opposed Calmar but there was a certain amount of coldness towards him with glances and whispers that he could not miss. Any illness in Camp Pole and Colban was asked for, he refused to come saying he trusted Calmar, but Calmar knew this was happening. People didn't consult him about anything, preferring Colban's advice, but Colban still insisted that those from camp Pole should go to Calmar.

Then came the time when, although the winter hasn't finished with the land, there is the early stirring of spring. The doe are in milk and the young are born. The day came when the sky was blue and clear and the Sun shone and there was a frost on the grass.

The holy men brought their people to the temple. Colban had brought a new breed of cow in calf up the valley that appeared to be somewhat tame and willing to be led.

"Behold." He called out. "No longer must we go and hunt in the hills for all our meat. This is the first of a new type of cattle which we can keep near us and breed and raise ourselves. I have arranged for more to come in a few days. This is the dawning of a new way of life for us all."

"You are taking the spears from the hands of our hunters. If we have meat here they are no longer hunters but tame like this cow." Said Calmar.

"No, indeed, both of our camps have stayed the same for many years now yet they must grow and you know we cannot always rely on the deer or the boar being where they should be. These we will always have near us. The hunters will still hunt, this cattle is simply a help when hunting is hard."

"This is only the start, you have other plans. You are making our people tame."

"The world is changing, Calmar, we change and grow with it or get swept away. Other camps are growing, they will come here and take over unless we grow and learn the new ways too, for if they grow and see we do not they will look at our valley with greedy eyes, they will outnumber us and we will not be able to defend ourselves. You spend too much time looking inward and have never been beyond the valley, you need to look beyond and see the world. It is not always the nice safe place we would wish it to be. I am not making our people tame but preparing them for threats from outside."

There was a lot of movement among the people, some uneasy mutterings. For all the trust they had in Colban it did seem as if he was taking something away from the hunters.

"I asked Colban to help with this." Said Tharon. "Our traders have seen these cattle in other camps but no one was willing to trade. Colban has the oak crown and many camps have no holy man and his advice and aid was the only way anyone would trade this animal. Also our traders have had news of fighting between camps in distant places but it is getting closer, the world is changing. Besides, we will still need hunters but they will need to train to be warriors as well."

"You say not every camp has a holy man?" Said Calmar. "Then I will find someone who will appreciate me, I am obviously not wanted here. I will go to a people who are not being tamed, a people who can still hunt. I will go to a people who are not fooled by smooth words and who do not bow down to a tame goddess."

"Calmar, this is your place, this is your family and you are wanted." Tharon assured him. "You have got us all wrong, and Moonpool is certainly not tame either."

Calmar looked around at the people. There was no move from anyone else to beg him not to go. He sought out Sarak and when he saw him he thought of appealing to him but he kept his eyes down and shuffled uneasily with his feet.

"My mind is made up Colban, you can have all these people to yourself. This is what you wanted all along." He glared at Sarak and one or two others who he thought would be on his side but none of them responded. "Did I not warn you this was his intention? Slowly he has manipulated you and wormed his way into your lives. Now he frightens you with tales of attack."

Still no one moved. Calmar knew he had backed himself into a corner and he had no choice but to gather his things together and stride off towards the west hoping some camp would welcome him.

When he left many of the people wished him well and gave him little trinkets but no one tried to persuade him to stay. He did expect some of his family and friends to go with him and when he went it was alone and it was with great bitterness.

Chapter 14

Innovation

Every evening Tharon and Ralton stood in the temple to watch the Sun go down, sometimes they spoke but mostly they stood in silence waiting. I could see concern in their eyes, they were the leaders of two camps whose ancestors were considered wise, and they had settled here and made a successful foundation for the people who followed. They both felt the responsibility of following their example and neither were sure of their own wisdom and ability to guide. The world was changing and their camps needed to change and grow, the future was uncertain. There was also a certain amount of distrust between the camps despite their joint heritage, Calmar had caused a rift, even though he was gone he had put doubts in people's minds and many of them were close family of his. And how were they to defend their people if they were attacked, they knew about hunting but if other people came with weapons what were they to do?

"Oh, Moonpool." Ralton called out to me. "You have always been here, you knew Ban and you have protected and guided us through so many leaders. Tell us, how do we face the future, how do we guide our people? How do we protect them?"

This was such an earnest request and I was moved by it. So I stood with them quietly so they hardly noticed I was there until I spoke.

"Ralton, your camp is high, it is dry and there is plenty of wood, in this valley is clay in abundance, learn the art of firing pots like those Colban and Calmar had. Tharon, the land round your camp is lush and fairly flat and easily cleared, breed the cattle. The two camps need each other. There are other new things coming too, learn of them and discover what you are good at. Neither of you are any less capable than all who have gone before. As your traders travel let them learn of defence and prepare."

"And you will protect us?"

"I will keep peace in the valley as much as I can. Your people are quite capable of protecting themselves if you only trust them. With the new things they will learn the camps will grow."

Having quietly said my peace I felt the rest was up to them. And I was gone.

They looked at each other and I don't know what they were most startled by, my brief appearance or the simplicity of the advice.

In any case, they took my advice. Ralton sent people to learn the art of firing pots and they set up a workshop and a kiln and were soon making fine pots which were so very useful to both camps as well as an extra trade item. Tharon sent Colban with several people to trade for more cattle and to learn how to manage them and there was soon a sizeable heard grazing on the land about the camp. Neither camp had to lose their skill as hunters, the deer still came and went, the cattle needed protection from predators, the only difference being that they had to be careful when they followed the deer into the higher ground as camps were beginning to spring up all over and much of their old hunting grounds were considered someone's territory. The traders also brought many new skills and the hunters began to train as fighters by sparing against each other.

Both villages grew, though Ban's village grew the most as there was more room and better land.

Over the years Colban had observed the phases of the Moon and the range of the Sun and had placed posts in the temple to mark significant events, he said this was important to understand the seasons better for managing the cattle and the cutting and drying of grass for winter feed. He also said it would be more important for what was to come.

The Earth rolled on and on. Ralton's grandson had a son, Barnel, and a daughter who he named Rainbow. Colban, by now very old, took Rainbow in his arms and brought her to the temple. There before the gathered people he lifted her high above the altar as the sun rose in the east and proclaimed.

"Here is my successor, the blood of Little Rainbow and Ban run almost pure in her veins so she will be greater than me."

He was right. As she grew I could see both Little Rainbow and Ban in her. She was bright and happy and wise beyond her years and when she was old enough was sent to the Oak Thicket for training. The Thicket may be only just beyond my valley's limits but it could be another world for all I know about it, even among our kind it is a closely guarded secret.

The seasons came and went very many more times before Rainbow returned. She also had won the prestigious oak crown. She had also acquired from somewhere in the west five and three creature with a woollen fleece which were driven along by a domesticated dog, these were my first sight of the sheep that I had heard much of. She brought them to the open space between the eastern end of the temple and the river. People from both villages gathered, bringing Colban on a bench on the shoulders of five and one men, to welcome Rainbow and marvel at the new creatures.

They set Colban down in the temple.

"Let me touch Rainbow." He said in a weak voice.

She came and knelt before him. His eye had become weak and he could hardly see so as he reached out his hand he had to search for her a moment and felt for her forehead.

"Bless you, Rainbow, you will be greater than I and you will bring changes for the good. I know the bleating I hear is some new creature you have brought but you have other ideas too. I may not be able to see with my eyes but I can see clearly much of what is to come. Now I may die in peace."

He slumped down, his breathing was shallow. The people watched over him until the Sun was about to set and he quietly slipped away with one last long breath.

"Farewell wise Colban." Said Rainbow. "We will bury you here that you may continue to watch over us."

Fires were lit in bowls and placed around his body and people brought small tokens of beads and antler knives and woven charms. Over the passing of the seasons Colban had healed the rifts by his kind and gentle manner and the people loved him deeply. They were determined they would do whatever was necessary to honour his legacy in the ceremony of his funeral. Wood was brought and piled all around him and his body was burned there in the enclosure and the fire lit the night sky, the sparks flying up and seeming to mingle with the stars as if his very being was being taken up to be with them. And in the morning as the Sun soared up into the sky his ashes and bones were buried before the stone altar and the people raised a chant to him.

In the afternoon Rainbow selected five and five and two people from the combined camps and lead them, with the sheep, up to the hill to the west between two branches of the valley where she instructed them on how to look after the sheep, how to cut the wool and how to weave it into clothes. She placed her nephew Vellon in charge of this new camp.

So, now there were three camps and still one people, the temple brought them together for every special occasion, Rainbow made sure of this. She celebrated every significant phase of the Moon, every important position of the Sun, every joining of man and woman and the birth of their children and every passing of a soul into the west.

Chapter 15

Stones

One night when the Moon was full Rainbow stood in the western entrance of the temple and gazed at the Moon's reflection in the river. The flow of the river caused her image to waver and dance and break into pieces and as she moved across the sky after a while her reflection disappeared into the bank. Even after the reflection had gone Rainbow stood and gazed at the rippling water. She was deep in thought and I could see she wasn't sure of the best way to go with something.

I stood behind her and waited with her. I felt strongly the kinship with Little Rainbow and the pain in my heart was as strong as it had always been, for our kind do not forget but can relive a memory as if it happened now. It is never easy for me to be in human form but there are times, like this, when it is necessary. Times when the humans find it hard to say in words what is in their heart and mind without there being a physical presence they can actually acquaint with and talk directly to. So much of their communication is based on the reaction of someone and much is unspoken anyway.

"Moonpool." She whispered, hoping I would come, not yet aware I was already there.

"Rainbow." I whispered back.

She sighed.

We both stood silent, she wanted to ask me something and wasn't sure how to ask or if she even ought to ask, that much I could tell. I have waited while The Maker Of All Things formed the earth. I was there as he made the ice roll to and fro across the land, so this was not a burden to me. I could wait. But if nothing happened soon it would be dawn and we would not have the quiet for her to ask what she so desperately wanted to ask. So I moved beside her and took her hand.

"Moonpool." She said at last. "This is your quiet place and you have allowed us to invade it over and over again."

I squeezed her hand. "This is as much a quiet place for your people, you do not invade rather you honour me. If I really want quiet I do not take on human form where I can float with the breeze and dance with the sunlight."

"In many places like this people are placing stones where the wooden posts are now."

"Yes, I know. This is what you have wanted to ask of me isn't it? You want my permission to do this, but not that you really need it you have my permission. You will also have my help."

"Your help?"

"Even with all the people of the villages it will not be easy to move the stones from the mountains, once you get them to a river it would be easier but these stones need to come over the mountain. The blue stones you are thinking of, I can make them lighter for the journey."

"You can?" She was quite taken aback by this.

"How do you think so many stones have been moved already to different sites if not with the help of my people?"

"You mean ..."

"They will still be heavy and will need a lot of people to move them, but you will need a few stones and we don't want to wear everyone out do we. I will need Preseli's permission to come into his mountains and you will need gifts for the people there. Sheep and cattle and pots will do, mostly sheep, cattle don't do so well on the mountains."

She turned to face me. "You have already thought this through."

"You were silent a long time, I had time to think."

"You knew what I was going to ask?"

"As I said, I know this is what others are doing, it made sense that you were thinking about it too."

Preseli was more than happy, his people don't have many sheep and they can't eat stones. I enjoyed immensely walking with the group of five and five and five and five men and five and five and three women up to the extreme west of my valley and then following the main valley up into the north and from there up into the mountains, leading a large flock of sheep and a few cattle. There is a lot of joy among the humans when they get together to do something practical and important and they share many things when they travel together. For the whole journey I almost felt like one of them and when their minds drifted from who I was they treated me as such. Humans may have a spiritual side but they are very much bound to the physical and anything beyond what they can see doesn't always occupy any part of their thought.

Preseli's people had already chosen some stones that were all very similar and the right size for what we wanted, they had done so for other groups before. We had taken a good quantity of trees that had already been cut into logs to slide the stones on since what trees did grow on the mountains were small and windswept. We unpacked our ropes made of plaited reeds, assigned five and five people to pull and one to move the logs which were laid as runners for the stones to slide along and to pour water on them to reduce friction, and so for each of three stones. I caused the stones to be a small amount of their actual weight and we set off back over the mountain and down to the river where we floated the stones on the logs.

We went back three more days so we had sufficient stones for the temple. Others had dug holes for the stones as Rainbow directed and with great care they tipped the stones end on into the holes. When all was done we all stood back and viewed the result from the sunrise end and the sunset end, we wouldn't know for sure until we had seen the Sun and the Moon rise and set in all the important times but I knew Rainbow was exact in her positioning. There would be no need to move any of them so I caused the stones to be their true weight again.

That night there was celebrating and feasting and singing and dancing and I was gone quietly before this. This had been a joy for me but I am other than them, this event only deepened a longing in me and I needed time to be spirit only and put feelings away.

I sought Silverwheel.

"Was I wrong in being with them for so long?"

"It was not wrong. Humans are strange as you probably found, it is possible to walk among them and even if they know who you are they don't seem to know all the time. Even I don't understand this."

"It won't affect their development will it?"

"No, they are in much the same place they would have been anyway. They wanted the stones in the temple. You just made it easier for them and they were able to accomplish it in just three days."

I was silent for a while.

"But was it a mistake for me?" I asked. "I have seen my actions have consequences and I am not sure the consequences have been good or bad."

"More and more people will come to your valley, to watch over them you need to understand them. You need to know how they think, and you need to know how they view you."

"I did have fun though. Was that wrong?"

"Fun, joy, you are a nature spirit it is part of who you are and the more fun and joy there is in the valley the more fun and joy the inhabitants will have, it will diffuse into them just by their being here. There will be sadness enough, enjoy the now." She regarded me silently for a moment. "As for consequences, you think that by confronting Por it eventually led to all that happened with Little Rainbow."

"Well it did."

"Sprites are notoriously headstrong. This was bound to happen at some time as the mortals fill the land. You are not responsible for her actions. Besides look at the good that has come of it, you miss the lake but the people are closer without it between them. And look at the good the temple has been for them which would never have been if the land was still at the bottom of the lake."

"But even so ..."

"We are nature spirits, more closely bound to the humans than the higher spirits. Our destiny is interwoven with theirs in ways I do not know, yours more than mine. I travel round the earth and see much but am not as close to humanity as you are, enjoy that closeness and the experiences it brings."

Chapter 16

Gathering

Rainbow was the first to wake the next morning just before the Sun rose, the air was clear and the stars began to fade as the sky brightened in the east. She stood just outside the temple on the bank of the river and gazed down at the swirling waters. This was the point at which it was safe to cross, from this point the traders took to boats and paddled down all the way to the sea and the large settlement where the river was tidal.

The temple was complete, she had inspired all the people with her plan and they had something they could all be proud of. Yet something was still bothering her. She was such a restless soul and had to be planning or doing something new all the time.

"Moonpool." She said

"Rainbow." I was there beside her.

"We are on an island. Not just you and me, here. I mean the whole land. We know of the sea to the west and the south, it also goes all the way round far to the east and north into the cold and dark."

"Yes, now we are, it was not always so. Also it is not always cold and dark in the far north."

"Do you know the place of the Great Gathering in the centre of the island?"

"I know of it." I also knew it was not at the centre of the island but I didn't correct her on this because a great many believed it was.

"I would like some of our younger people to attend the Great Gathering this year at the summer solstice. Apart from trading the people here have little idea of the greater world, it would do them good to mix with people beyond those they can possibly know, to share ideas and to learn what else there is. Do you mind?"

"Why would I mind? I do not own the people, they are free to come and go as they wish. I also think it is a good idea."

"And another thing, I would like to invite people from other villages in this area to gather here for the solstice, would that be alright?"

"Of course. Why would it not?"

"I know this is your special place and we are always intruding on it."

"This is a thin place where the separation between realities is at its weakest. Ever since the lake drained away I have had to come to terms with the whole valley as being my special place. I do not have to come here to speak to my kind, but I still find that peace here when I am alone that makes it easier, everything that has happened here has not interfered with that. Whatever happens, because the Otherworld is close here it will always be a place of peace. I am glad that people find this place special since you are spirit as well as physical, I am glad to share it with you."

"Oh." She looked at me quizzically. "I never thought of you talking to others of your kind, I realise they are everywhere but it just hadn't occurred to me. You must think me really stupid. I always thought you must be either very lonely or not needing to talk to your own kind."

In fact I talk to them all the time but this tale is more about the humans than us, we do not change much over time and it would not make a story.

Several days before the solstice a party of five and three of the younger members of the three camps got together, with pots and skins and wool to trade and plenty of dried meat for the journey, and they set off down the valley. The earth spun a few more times and people from many other camps in the area began to arrive and set up temporary shelter on the flat ground to the east of the temple.

Many of the cattle and sheep were killed. The hunters brought in several wild boars, all to feed the growing encampment. Those who came also brought produce, there was deer from the high country, bread made from cultivated grains in the lowlands, fish from the sea, cheeses of various sorts, drinks from fermented grains, there was honey collected from bees and all manner of root vegetables.

There was noise, laughter, music, dancing all the time. There were drums, hollow horns that could be blown through to make different tones, tough reeds with holes that tunes could be played on. The clothes were varied as many different materials were becoming available, woven reeds, wools as well as skins, colours from berries and insects of different sorts. There was jewellery of woven reeds and bones small stones and fired clay.

I found I could walk among them mostly unnoticed, with such a varied selection of peoples and dress I could blend in. Unnoticed in that the visitors did not know who I was but I did tend to attract the attention of many of the men, I hadn't given much attention to my looks before. Although I had at times glanced at my reflection in the lake when it was still there and I saw that my features were much finer than any of the humans. As I walked through the crowds I was given all sorts of food and drink, but as I need neither I always managed to quietly leave these somewhere when asked to dance. Dancing was such fun and so much of nature is rhythm and movement, all the men I danced with commented on my ability but when you have seen the dance of the stars and the planets this is simply nature. I hoped all this attention wouldn't make me vain.

One man, tall and rugged and quite handsome, seemed to be somewhere near to me all the time, watching and waiting. Eventually he moved towards me.

"Hello." He said, offering me a small bowl of the liquid of fermented grain. "My name is Tallon, what is your name."

"Moonpool."

"What a lovely name, it really suits you." He touched my cheek. "And where are you from, I have never seen you before." His speech was slightly slurred, something that happens with these beverages.

"Oh, I live here."

“Then you should make me welcome. “

He was as transparent as they come. There is something base and less than animal at times with humans. Their own opinions of themselves and the assumptions they make about others. I stepped back, away from him, his breath I found quite offensive.

“Now, come on, I am Tallon of the Sea Port.” And he lunged at me to grab me.

I grabbed his wrists and, strong though he was for a human, held him there.

“I am Moonpool of this valley.” I said calmly.

He looked down at his wrists where I held them, amazed that he couldn’t move them in the slightest, I am flower and grass and tree and soil and rock, and he could no more move the hills than my hands.

I dropped his wrists and I was gone.

Early the next morning just before the Sun rose over the hill Rainbow had gathered everyone together in and around the temple, everyone except Tallon and one or two others who were sleeping off the effects of the previous day in their temporary shelters.

All was silent. It seemed as if everyone was holding their breath. Rainbow began the chant with her soft sweet voice. Slowly the sky brightened in the east and a low murmur came from the gathered people as they joined the chant. Then there came the bright flash of the sun’s first rays and a roar came from the many throats that rose to a deafening shout as the Sun heaved himself slowly above the horizon. The light formed a beam between a perfectly aligned gap in the stones that passed right through the temple and this was the sign for the merriment to really begin. If the people had been merry before they were ecstatic now.

Rainbow then lead a procession of dancers following the beam and then round the top of the bank, they had drums and horns and whistles, they sang to the god of the Sun and to The Maker Of All Things. I had told Rainbow to leave me out of this as I was only a lesser spirit, but some of my people raised a chorus to me anyway. I did wonder how Tallon would feel if ever this was reported back to him.

The procession continued to dance and sing back to the temporary camp where celebrations began again.

A weak voice from Tallon's shelter called out, "Go away, keep the noise down." And this only incited the revellers to laugh and shout and blow their horns.

Rainbow stayed behind in the temple. She placed a bowl on the stone filled with herbs and flower petals.

"This is for you Moonpool. I do not know what else to give to express my thanks."

She dropped to her knees for a moment before standing and following the others.

I stood alone and unseen and took the bowl in my hands, I breathed in the scents of the herbs and the petals and I sighed. This gift touched me in its simplicity. I could not take it with me and I sighed again and placed it back on the stone and even shed a tear and before all the emotion flooded in I was gone.

Chapter 17

Return

The people who came to us slowly left the next day, new friendships had been made, agreements between clans, new things learned and exchanged, new parings between men and women.

Rainbow stood again outside the temple and gazed down the river, there is something in flowing water that seems to captivate people, as if it reminds them that even time is constantly flowing and taking them with it. Rainbow particularly was drawn to this possibly because she was so restless herself and always wanting to be on the move. She was on her own but I could feel that she wished for my presence so I stood with her.

"You did well, Rainbow, you brought many people together and everyone benefited."

She smiled a half smile. "All except Tallon of the Sea Port. He missed the sunrise and when he woke that afternoon he was asking if anyone had seen Moonpool, they all quite honestly said they hadn't. Of course no one wanted to explain who you were."

"You are very thoughtful, is something wrong?"

"There is something but I can't explain. I feel in my bones that I have missed something or made a mistake."

I didn't answer. This was something for her to sort out.

"Moonpool." She took her eyes of the river and looked directly at me. "You have always been here, you have seen so many people come and go. You know much more of the world than I do, have I missed something?"

"There are times when I feel the same as you especially when I get involved in human life. I could have just kept out of things. It would have been easier for me I will admit. But I choose to get involved and because of that I get caught up in the moment. Simply enjoy the moment, everything you have done has been good, accept that. Away from you my experience is that life goes on, events balance out, let the future take care of itself."

She smiled. "Enjoy the moment. Very well."

"Yes. If I may make an observation, you are never satisfied with having done something and you are always looking for the next great thing. Now is the time to do nothing."

The Sun rose and set and rose again two more times and there were shouts as the young people who had gone away had returned. There were two of those who had gone who hadn't returned and two new faces. Some matchings had been made and there would be new blood in the valley.

Barnel's son Hawkwind had led them there and back. He had a new, longer bow and arrows with smaller and more intricately shaped heads and highly coloured bird feather flights which he was keen to show everyone. He also had a domesticated dog that had been trained for running after the birds he shot and bringing them back. There were new styles in clothing and new tools for all sorts of things.

"What was the Great Gathering like?" Barnel asked him.

"The main temple was huge and the stones massive. There were other temples and villages all over the place. There were so many people there no one could count them, I had no idea the world was so big, it was so exciting. When we gathered to watch the Sun rise I almost cried with the emotion of it, you have no idea what it is like to be in such a huge crowd all chanting and shouting together."

Tholan, the son of Toban of camp Ban had also gone and he returned with a partner, Jenn. They had brought a large woven bag filled with seeds and a large piece of antler chosen to break up the ground.

"Jenn's family are skilled at growing grain and making bread." Explained Tholan. "We are going to try this here."

"That is good." Said Toban. "But what else did you see there."

"There are so many holy sites there, not only the main temple. I think they have many gods but mainly they worship the Sun and the Moon and a great god called Woden. We saw many men who are there only to build, they do not need to hunt or work on the land or with the animals. But I am glad to be back, it was too busy there and you are just one among so many, here we have meaning, we are important."

"Their holy man was very interested in us when he learned where we were from." Said Redfire, cousin to Tholan. "He was asking about the blue stones we have, they have some there which have been taken there by other families further north. He wanted to know if we were interested in trading ours."

"Trade with what?" Asked Toban. "You have brought many new things with you, and we have learned much from the people who came here, what more can there be?"

"He has many spells and magic and herbs. There are illnesses Rainbow cannot cure and he knows of herbs that can cure everything."

"And can he cure death itself?"

"No." Said Tholan. "That he can't, after all the main temple is also used for the ashes of all those who die there."

"There are many things he can do for us." Redfire persisted. "We don't really need these stones."

"We brought them here with great effort." Said Toban. "Even Moonpool helped."

"I know how much effort there was, but that was us, I saw no sign of Moonpool helping. She is only a local goddess anyway and there are greater gods at the Gathering. We are part of a larger world and shouldn't be hiding ourselves away."

Everyone went silent, Redfire must have realised he went too far.

"I just thought." He lowered his eyes and bowed his head a little. "There is more we can gain. But if you want to keep your stones that is up to you."

"It is not just that." Said Toban. "If he has all these spells and cures, why trade with our stones, why not give freely? If he can do so much good why not simply do so? Surely that is what holy people do."

Redfire had no answer to this.

Later that day as the Sun sank into the west Toban, Barnel and Vellon along with Rainbow gathered in the large round hall in Ban's camp that was used for meetings.

"There are so many new things." Said Toban. "In one way it is exciting but also I must admit I am a little fearfull."

"Change is the way of the world." Said Vellon.

"The world doesn't change." Said Rainbow. "The seasons come and go, the Sun moves up in the sky and down again. We learn more and more about the world all the time, it is us who are changing."

"I have never known so many changes. I cannot always keep up." Toban sighed. "The world belongs to our children, is it time for us to step aside?"

"What worries me," Admitted Barnel. "Is that this holy man wants our stones. Why ours?"

"The stones aren't absolutely vital to us." Rainbow said quietly, her face sad. "But they represent the unity of the three camps, when we came together to bring them here it was important for all of us."

"And what did Redfire mean he didn't see Moonpool helping?" Said Tholan. "And to call her only a local goddess, she has protected and watched over our people since the time of Ban, what have the gods of the Gathering done for us? The Sun and the Moon are there for everyone, Moonpool cares for us alone."

"Redfire is only your cousin." Said Barnel. "He will not be chief, he wishes to be important and he has seen an opportunity but he is one voice only."

"But Moonpool, did he really not see her or didn't he want to. What do you think Rainbow?"

Rainbow thought for a moment. "I don't know why she appears at some times and not others, we have seen her a lot but I don't think this has always been the case. Perhaps it depends on our ability to see her and maybe Redfire genuinely can't, or he saw her but just assumed she was one of the people from another camp he hadn't met before. His may be only one voice now but I fear for the future. I worry that it may not have been wise to send our young people to the Great Gathering but we cannot hide ourselves away, if the world is changing then we need to embrace change. We cannot keep the world out and hide ourselves away."

She sighed, this was probably what had been bothering her before, humans are able to see dimly into the future at times but very rarely realise they can.

"Let the future take care of itself." She repeated my words.

Chapter 18

Dwindling

The seasons came and went. Every year the young went east to the Great Gathering for the summer solstice and every year fewer came back. Every year there was a gathering here but in every visiting group there were fewer people. It wasn't just our young who were leaving. Having opened up the world to them they were being tempted away from all over.

Rainbow, now older, stiffer and her hair whiter, stood silently in the temple before dawn though the sky was overcast and she would not be able to see the Sun and unusually for her not watching the river. In a strangely significant way the weather was matching her mood. It was no special occasion, no position of the Sun or the Moon, and it was not a funeral or a binding of man and woman so she was alone. I felt a deep sadness in her and I was reluctant to appear even though in her soul she was reaching out to me. Yet so deep was her longing for me that I relented.

"Rainbow." I said as I stood beside her.

There was a sadness that was intense. We felt the drain of people to the east as a slow death of the villages here. In her younger days everything had been so bright and positive, she was supposed to be the greatest holy woman of the valley. In those days she had felt she was doing so much good, but not now.

"Moonpool. I am so sorry."

"Sorry? For what?"

"I thought I was doing something to help the communities but people are being drawn away. I have tried to stop them taking your stones but I am afraid there is too much pressure from the Great Gathering and soon they will go. I hope everyone doesn't drift away but how can these villages survive with fewer and fewer people. My time is drawing to an end now and I do wonder what I have actually accomplished."

"The villages themselves are not important they are only buildings, the people will live on wherever they go. Whatever else you have done you helped them see beyond their small world here and they will do well in the greater world."

"But if everyone goes you will be on your own."

"I have been here on my own a long time and humans from my perspective are still new. All things come and go. I have enjoyed the human company for this short time and I have learned much and am richer for it and I have my memories. Don't worry about me. I will be here if and when I am needed."

"I'm sorry that they are calling you a local goddess after all you have done for us. They have forgotten how much they owe you."

"Well I am only a local spirit, I am not important in the order of things. There are things happening beyond this island that even those at the Great Gathering have no idea about and even Woden is only a small spirit in the greater world let alone beyond this world. We are all lower beings than even the messengers of The Maker Of All Things."

"Then I'm sorry that sometimes I forget who you are."

"Already I fade but it is only this body you see, the valley remains and will remain and therefore I remain. Does it matter that only you can see me? You remind me so much of Little Rainbow and it breaks my human heart to think you will go soon."

I looked around at the valley, not all of it you could see from where we stood. The clouds blew away, the sky cleared and the Sun broke in glory above the hills.

"This valley remains." I said after a long deep breath. "Humans may leave for the moment but they will need this valley again and I will be here."

Rainbow died soon after and her ashes were buried by the entrance to the temple. Not for many cycles of the seasons but eventually the stones were moved. Large rafts were made and the stones were loaded onto them and floated down the river, perhaps I should have helped but I wasn't asked and so they had the full weight to contend with.

Many people left but not all. The three camps survived, Storban son of Tholan led camp Ban, Dawnlight daughter of Hawkwind led camp Pole and Eagle son of Vellon led Vellon's camp. Malnor, Storban's brother, was holy man for the three camps and he continued to hold vigils at the thin place for the important times of the year and for the cremations of the dead and the joining of men and women. They spoke of me but not to me, but I watched over them.

The growing of grain for bread never succeeded but they grew many other things such as new strains of root vegetables and cultivated fruit trees. The sheep and cattle did well and camp Pole continued to make clay vessels. They still hunted deer and boar and they still traded. Some of them still went to the Great Gathering but as many returned as went though not always the same people, pairings were made at the Gathering and life went on for the humans.

Chapter 19

Reawakening

The earth moved on round and round the Sun. The seasons came and went and the camps began to grow again. The line of Ban didn't fail and his blood and the blood of Little Rainbow still flowed in their veins. Much strength was brought in to the family lines from outside and because of the contact with the greater world their learning increased.

Somehow I found myself able to take on human form and I stood in the thin place again as the sun rose like it did all those times before. I looked round at the valley. Much of it had been cleared of trees and cattle filled the lowland and sheep the hills. I enjoyed the moment, the sights, the smells, the warmth of the sun, the gentle breeze, the soft grass and the rich soil under my feet.

"Hello." Said a small voice behind me. "Are you Moonpool?"

A girl of about three years stood at the entrance. Her dark hair was thick and wild, her blue eyes intently staring at me.

"Yes, I am Moonpool. And you are Sunlight of camp Ban."

"You know me?"

"You know me too."

"Everyone knows about Moonpool."

"Everyone knows about me but only you know me. Thank you."

It was because of the childish innocence of this girl that I could take on human form after so long. I may still not fully comprehend the passing of time but I realised in this instance that I had missed human contact.

"Can you do magic?"

"You could call it magic, I am nature and if you like all of nature is magic." I took a dry branch in my hand and it sprouted leaves, I gave it to her. I waved a hand and the dew leapt up from the grass and caused a rainbow in the air.

Sunlight jumped up and down with glee and tried clapping her hands but the branch made it difficult. "I'm going to tell my father." She started running back to the camp, stopped and turned for a moment. "I can come and see you again? You will be here?" And off she ran.

The next day she returned. I was standing just breathing in the air, remembering the people I had been close to. I allowed my heart to feel, it may be calm without a human heart but I did miss the feelings, the joys and the sorrows and I smiled. Although there was a lot of pain which would not go away there was a lot of love too. And I was eager to gain new experiences from this lively little girl.

"I'm back." She called as she bounded down the track to the thin place.

"On your own again? Your father isn't with you?"

"No one believed me, but I don't care. I wanted to see you again anyway."

"I'm glad you're here. It has been so long and you make me feel young."

"My mother is coming I think, she didn't believe me but she wants to keep an eye on me. She told me not to enter the holy place."

"You can come in. Nothing is going to hurt you, nothing is forbidden."

"Sunlight! Sunlight!" Called a woman from some distance.

"My mother." She said and ran back to meet her.

I followed her. Sunlight had grabbed her mother's hand and was pulling her along.

"Hello." Said Jaren, her mother. "Has Sunlight been bothering you? You aren't from around here."

"No bother at all, in fact she has been very helpful."

"Have you travelled far?"

We continued to walk back to the thin place.

"No." I said. "I have always been here."

"I don't remember you from any of the villages round here, are you from over the hill?"

We arrived at the thin place and I started to walk in.

"No!" Said Jaren. "The spirit of Ban is there, this is a place of the dead, only Tamlin may enter."

"You still remember Ban, Jaren?"

"You know me?"

"I knew Ban too. You may enter since it is not a place of the dead but of the living."

Jaren was silent, I could see her mind was working, was she sure she heard what I just said? Almost against her will Sunlight led her to the entrance of the thin place.

"Show us some magic, Moonpool." Pleaded Sunlight.

"I don't want to shock your mother as she doesn't think I'm Moonpool."

"Then you must show us some magic so she knows."

"Jaren, do not be shocked by this." I warned.

Such was the simple belief of Sunlight that not only was I visible to her mother but I was able to display my wings as well. I am proud of my wings and don't get to display them often, huge and dark and almost transparent so the sun can shine through them. Jaren was open mouthed for a moment then fell to her knees and Sunlight was filled with glee and danced and clapped round me.

"Your pardon, Moonpool. I did not know. We didn't think you were real, we thought you were only a story."

"I am a story, but I am also real. Stand up, come in and sit with me a while."

I folded my wings. Sunlight came up to me and took my hand, Jaren, rather stunned, followed tentatively. We went to one side and sat on the bank.

"This is not a place of death it is a place of life." I repeated. "It symbolises the cycle of everything, it is a gateway to the Otherworld so only the remains of the physical bodies are here."

Jaren reached for a metal pin she had in her woollen cloak. "For this honour I must give you this." She unfastened it and gave it to me.

I turned it over in my hand and held it up to the light of the sun. "So this is bronze, it is quite beautiful."

It was a small disc with a hooked pin that could be fastened to clothing. Jaren had it because she was of the ruling family. I knew the ruling families were gathering all sorts of goods including small items of bronze when they could trade for them, they had become somewhat separated from the other people of their communities and could demand tribute from them. In some places there were items made of rarer metals like gold. I offered it back.

"I cannot take this." I said apologetically. "I am not always in this form so I would have nowhere to fasten it to."

Reluctantly she took it.

"You have an older son, Wolfclaw, he will be chief."

"I should not be sitting here alongside you." She kept her head bowed. The implication of who I was left her stunned.

"Sunlight will soon go to the Oak Thicket to learn to be a holy woman, she is very bright."

"Oh, no." Jaren looked briefly at me before blushing and looking down at the ground again. "There is no one there. The Teacher hasn't been there as long as anyone remembers, we thought he was a story too, but if you are real then he must be. Holy ones only learn from holy ones."

She started folding and unfolding her hands, there was something that had occurred to her in that moment, a request that she didn't dare make. Sunlight was getting fidgety until she could stand it no longer, the same thought had occurred to her. Suddenly she jumped off the bank and stood facing me. Children can be very perceptive and very quick, and doubt and caution very rarely get in the way.

"Moonpool, you can teach me."

Jaren blushed and cleared her throat and continued to look down at the ground. “It is much to ask.” I wasn’t sure if she said this to me or to Sunlight.

“It is indeed.” I said, reflecting. “I do not know what the Teacher taught as the Oak Thicket was a hidden place even to me.”

“You are a goddess.” Jaren looked directly at me, a mother brave enough to ask anything for her daughter. “You know all things.”

“I know a great many things but I do not know all things.”

“Oh please Moonpool, it will be so much fun.” Said Sunlight jumping up and down, so enthusiastic was she it was hard to resist.

“I would be glad to teach you what I can.” I jumped off the bank and took Sunlight’s hands and we danced round and round.

Jaren just sat in silence. This was so much for a mortal mind to take in so suddenly.

Chapter 20

Learning

In the night we stood at the point just outside the thin place where you can see the Moon reflecting on the river. It was not the same as the lake but it still brought back the memory of my first meeting with a human. Because the river flowed and swirled the image wavered and danced and sparkled, I knew Silverwheel smiled and in that smile I knew I had her consent.

"To me it only seems a short time but to you it is a long, long time ago." I began. "Where we are standing was under a vast lake so back up the hill a way there your distant father, Ban, came to the lake and saw the Moon reflected as you see it now, but the lake was still and vast and the reflected Moon didn't waver and it appeared to be deep in the lake. Then the first word I ever heard spoken by a human was Moonpool and so I was named from that moment. I had my doubts when the lake disappeared, which I will tell you about later, but Ban called me Moonpool and Moonpool I will always be."

She looked intently at me. "Moonpool." She repeated. "Yes, you are Moonpool."

I told her about the Moon and the Sun and their chase across the sky, how the Moon is stronger at her furthest from the Sun. I told her of their yearly trek up and down the sky that governed the seasons. I told her about the stars and their groupings and their stories and the songs they sang and she assured me that she could hear them.

The seasons came and went and Sunlight grew and soaked up all the learning. I taught her about all growing things and the importance of the herbs. I taught her about all animals and their relationships with the humans.

We wandered far and wide throughout the valley where we uncovered the secret hiding places of the mice and the insects, the badgers and the foxes and the hares. We sought out the rare plants and the best times to gather them. I taught her about the herbs and their uses in healing and in preparing food and we gathered and dried them and stored them for when they were needed.

The people of the valley would stop what they were doing when we passed, we became a regular sight. I don't know who they thought I was, perhaps some holy woman from away who had come to instruct Sunlight. They never saw me appear and disappear as Sunlight always came to meet me at the holy place, and even when they came for festivals and celebrations Sunlight and I would already be there waiting.

Not even Tamlin knew who I was but realised I knew so much more than he did and was glad that I was the one teaching Sunlight since he didn't have the patience. He was willing for Sunlight to aid him in all the ceremonies, she was an extra pair of steady hands as he was a bit nervous and tended to drop things.

She learned to cure many illnesses and she helped deliver a few babies until it was I who helped her.

Tamlin was glad of this too as delivering babies was something he hated.

I taught her the history of her people. I taught her something of the wider world as well. I told her about how wonderful and grand and noble humans can be and did not hide how cruel and greedy and base they can be too. I told her about how they can come together to do great works and how they can fight and kill for land and possessions and sometimes for no better reason than they don't believe the same things as each other.

Wisdom I could not teach but I was glad to discover that she had this though it was veiled in a sense of fun. In many ways she remained the young girl she was when I first met her and people found this disarming, they would naturally open up to her before they realised she was telling them something important.

Nor could I teach her about the human heart for though mine was human enough when in physical form I still did not understand my feelings for Ban after all that had gone. Nor why there was a deep yearning for something I knew not what. Nor my loss when Little Rainbow became fully human and the devastation I felt when the lake drained away. Nor why I felt like a little girl when with Sunlight.

One night I sat with Silverwheel in the enclosure gazing up at the Moon and I asked her.

"I'm not sure I fully understand either. You and I are only able to take on human form here at this time because of Sunlight's unfaltering belief in us. Only in our natural form we are truly ourselves, we are guardians and lesser spirits. But our ability to take on human form depends so much on the beliefs of someone it is almost as if we are made in their image while still retaining the essence of ourselves."

"I have noticed that humans do that too, even though being human is their natural state, they do to a certain extent reflect those they are with."

"Enjoy your time with Sunlight, it is your chance to feel young and dare I say you need this after so long without any human contact at all. Also I am glad you are being open about your feelings with her for Ban and Little Rainbow."

I reflected for a moment. "About Little Rainbow. I am still unsure; did I cause the collapse of the waterfall and the loss of the lake? Did The Maker Of All Things really bring her soul to be with him as he does with the humans?"

"These are questions we will never be able to answer only He knows and when you ask Him questions like that He will only say it is not for us to know."

"And what of the Teacher at the Oak Thicket? Why is he not there to teach?"

"Because people stopped going there. If Sunlight had gone there not even she could wake him, her belief is in you and therefore in me also, it is not in him."

"And who is teaching who here? I feel I am learning as much from Sunlight as I am teaching her."

"We are of nature and so are closer to the humans than the messengers, they do not change and grow but we do. You will grow with everyone whose life you share. You remember with Lia you could not appear in the day? This was because Ban named you for the night and so she believed you to be, you are still and will always be Moonpool whatever language people speak but you are also so much more."

We were both silent, breathing the air, listening to the sounds of life about us.

"One thing I fear." She said at last. "I circle the world and am above it, I am therefore so much more distant from people. But you are close to them and there is in you a deep yearning that you do not understand."

"I cannot hide anything from you can I? Is that something to fear then?"

"Yes. But I can say no more."

"Why?"

"No more, Moonpool. The Moon moves on and I must go."

The day came when I knew Sunlight was ready. It was the summer solstice and the people gathered to celebrate the Sun at his height. Tamlin was now too feeble and had left everything to me.

I stood at the end of the holy place where the Sun was rising and held aloft a crown of oak twigs plaited together. Sunlight knelt before me. I felt it best not to reveal who I was, let them think I was a holy woman from away and that was enough.

"People of the valley, behold Sunlight has completed her training. Let her be your holy woman, she will guide you and care for you, will you accept her and listen to her and help her in your turn?"

"We will." They said together.

"Sunlight. Do you accept the call of your people to be their holy woman? Will you care for them, tend their ills, help them in their disputes and gently guide them?"

"I will." She said, her eyes sparkling in the sunlight.

Placing the crown on her head I said. "Be the holy woman of the Valley by the authority I have to bestow."

She stood and turned to the people.

Wolfclaw approached with a woollen cloak and fastened it over her shoulders with a bronze clasp.

"Sunlight, receive my shared authority to lead the people." He said then returned to his place.

A young girl named Silverstar brought the bag of dried herbs I had given her for the occasion and she presented it to Sunlight.

"Sunlight, be our healer and our comfort in hard times." She said and returned to her place.

"It is done." I said. "These are your people and you their servant."

They all cheered and she was led away to the feast in Ban's camp that had been prepared. I stayed behind and was gone when no one was looking.

Chapter 21

Attack

Wolfclaw grew to be a strong leader. When his father died he came to the thin place at night and stood, gazing up at the Moon and the stars. He was very like his sister and was very open and willing to believe, probably the only other person who knew who I was. Responsibility weighed heavily on his shoulders but he was willing to seek advice. He knew of the unrest in neighbouring communities by listening to the traders and he feared for his own people. So he had come here not only to think and reflect but to ask for my help as well.

"Moonpool." He said quietly.

"Wolfclaw." I answered as quietly.

He turned to me and knelt. "You have been good to our people, you have been good to my sister and we have neglected you. You are goddess and we didn't even acknowledge you."

"You have lived in and cared for the valley and you have been a good people you have not neglected me."

"I know that an attack is coming. There are people who do not have such good land as us, people who feel their land is too small, people who want to rule over many."

I knew this too so I kept silent and waited for him to say more.

"I know I ask a great thing and I do not know how you relate to the other gods and goddesses but I ask your help for our defence. You are our goddess and you have always looked over us and protected us, will you protect us now?"

"More than anything you need to ask The Maker Of All Things for protection rather than me. I know where the first threat will come from but my brother over the hill has always resented that I was named Moonpool and he was Man On The Bush and that resentment he has instilled in the people who settled there. His people are bordered on the other side by a seafaring people who dwell on a tidal river and are more powerful than them. They are looking to expand so the obvious choice would be to overrun your villages and your land. They see you as soft and comfortable."

"We haven't had a lot to do with them, for we trade mostly with the east, especially the Sea Port. I often wondered why when it would be closer to trade with the Two River people."

"The Two River people are not easy to trade with as the Man On The Bush people know to their cost, they demand so much."

"Then why don't they trade with us? Surely that would better than thinking of attacking."

"People are not always rational."

"Anyway, Moonpool, can you help?"

"In your trading you have come across articles of bronze, you need some bronze arrowheads and some shields; I don't suppose you could get a bronze one. You need to keep a watch on all your borders as I cannot be certain that it will be from there that the first attack will come. In the past you have been generally on good terms with the people of the mountain as there has been a lot of beneficial trade for both sides, but theirs is a hard land and I cannot always read the hearts of humans."

"I have been training some of our hunters to be prepared, so when the alarm is sounded we will all gather in the one camp, whatever damage they do to the others we can repair if we are still here to do so. But is there anything else we need to do? However well prepared we are we will still need your protection, maybe you can prevent this happening at all."

"I cannot be seen to be interfering, I am only a nature spirit I have no authority over the free will of people. However, Bush is partly responsible so if I can help in an unobtrusive way who can blame me. I will try and reason with Bush but he can't be seen to be interfering either. And this I know, it will be soon."

And soon it was, the earth had turned only a few times and the people of the nearby villages made their move. When the attack came my people were prepared, even though the Bush people had persuaded the mountain people to join few though they were. Camp Ban had been enlarged and fortified and a wooden stockade built round it, the watchman on the hill blew his horn. Those who were to keep out of the fighting made their way up to Pole's camp as it was furthest away from the invaders while those who were to defend the valley gathered together in Camp Ban. They had amassed a large number of bronze tipped arrows, many shields including two with bronze plates nailed onto them.

Wolfclaw had even managed to acquire a long bronze sword.

The other spirits could not enter my territory without my permission and because we are strongest in our own land their people were on their own and all I had to do was not to be seen to be interfering. I know killing happens in nature and violence is a part of life and survival and I do not have a problem with that. But killing for no reason except greed and power I cannot abide. So if our defences were more impenetrable that they naturally should be and if the bronze tips of our arrows were faster and heavier than was usual I feel I was justified.

Still I was horrified at the violence on both sides. The number of people on both sides who were killed or badly wounded still troubles me. So much blood was shed and there was so much hatred in the air.

First there was a hail of arrows, many of the attackers were cut down in this first onslaught, they hadn't been ready for how prepared the defenders were and very few of their arrows got through the defences and no one inside was seriously wounded. Yet they pushed forward anyway and came to the stockade with ropes and ladders.

And when it came to actual contact with knives and axes and clubs the ferocity of the humans startled me. At least I could deflect as many blows to my people as I could but I cannot be everywhere at once. Wolfclaw was always in the thickest of the fighting and as much as possible I had to keep him alive.

The Sun passed its highest point and there was still hacking and smashing, I saw many of my people fall and I felt the loss of every one. Wolfclaw continued to fight bravely, with the stockade breached he left the relative safety of the camp and strode out into the enemy wielding his sword, his shield held firm before him, many fell by his hand. The attackers were not going to prevail and their losses were the greatest. If they didn't lay down their arms and beg for peace soon they would all be killed.

"Enough!" Shouted Sunlight.

It was truly amazing how quickly the fighting stopped and silence fell, apart from moaning and groaning from those seriously injured.

"Wolfclaw of Ban, Lomar of Pole, Greywing of Vellon, Strongwind and Sharpeye of the mountains, Barwood of Bush, come with me."

With that she strode off down the track to the thin place. There was no discussion, for a moment stunned silence then the men she had called one by one followed her.

Chapter 22

Peace

Sunlight sat on the bank where Ban's bones were and the others sat around, Wolfclaw, Lomar and Greywing sat together on one side and the aggressors on the other side.

"Barwood, what have you against us? Why come against us to kill us and take our land?" Asked Sunlight.

"Your people think they are special, you have been so busy trading in the east that you have had little to do with us, we have had no option but to deal with the people of the Two Rivers who are seafaring, they are extortionate to trade with. While you thrive we struggle." Said Barwood.

"What of the people to the south? Why not trade with them?"

"They have rich lands and they look towards the sea as well, they have the best of both worlds and do not trade with us, we have nothing they want."

"We are not an unreasonable people, you need not have attacked, if only you had tried but you keep yourselves to yourselves. That is no real answer you cannot justify what you have done. You say we have had little to do with you, why then have you not approached us? Strongwind and Sharpeye, I do not understand, we have always been on good terms with your people and have traded over the years."

"Ours is a hard land, we cannot grow crops and everyone has richer land for sheep and cattle." Said Strongwind. "Trade was good when we had something everyone wanted. You all wanted our stone, our axes and our arrowheads. But now you trade with metals and our future is unsure. You don't trade much with us now and once you stop trading with us the people of the north will also. What hope is there for our people, we need fertile land."

"Metal is rare." Said Sunlight. "You cannot build with metal. Look to the east, the Sea Port is growing, they need materials for building and stone endures longer than wood. They do not have much stone. Sharpeye may have sharp eyes but you do not have far seeing eyes, you only see need, you do not see opportunity. The world is larger than just us and the people of the north. That is not reason enough to come against us, tell us your concerns don't just attack."

"That is all very well." Shouted Wolfclaw, he jumped to his feet in frustration and anger. "You came against us to kill us and take our land for no reason at all, but you could not because we are too strong. Many of our people have been killed we demand justice."

"Many of our people have been killed too. Your losses were slight compared to ours." Barwood shouted back.

"Your people were killed and rightly so for you are the aggressor, we did not ask for this conflict, all your lives belong to us. If Sunlight hadn't stopped us you would all be dead now anyway."

"And more of our people would have died too." Said Lomar quietly. "Be grateful she stopped the fighting when she did. We have all suffered loss and yes Barwood is to blame and owes us a great debt which he can never repay but let the heat go out of the conflict. We are in a holy place here, can you not feel it?"

"Then Barwood at least should die. He is leader of his people and his is the responsibility. It is justice after all and let his death serve as a warning."

"We gain nothing by the death of anyone now nor can we bring back those who have died." Lomar continued. "We all have learned a hard lesson today. There are wrongs that cannot be righted no matter what we do and killing only leads to more killing. I fear that this will always be like a barrier between our people. We must try to find a way for peace between us or we will continue to come against each other and wipe each other out. We have lost many good people as have they and we will all struggle to recover and who knows, another people from further away will find our lands and benefit from our conflict, news of this will travel and there are stronger people beyond our lands who are looking to dominate. Isn't it better if we find a way to help each other?"

"Lomar speaks wisely." Said Greywing. "We all feel the loss deeply and the hurts between our peoples will run deep for years but now we need each other. Let Barwood live. The service he and his people can give us if he lives will be greater than if he dies, he owes us at the very least that much, if his life belongs to us then let his life benefit us."

"You hear that Barwood." Wolfclaw said in a moderated tone as he sat down. "We give you mercy but you owe us a debt."

Barwood could not answer. He was not in a position to argue, he didn't have enough surviving fighters even to protect his own land. This was a hard thing for him to accept but for the moment he had no choice.

"Then let us swear before Moonpool, Preseli, Man On The Bush and The Maker Of All Things that we will have peace. " Said Sunlight.

Such was the strength of her faith in us that it was almost as if the three of us were compelled to appear, although I was ready to do so anyway. And such was the shock of us appearing the leaders of the people slid off the bank and fell to their knees before us and swore there would be peace. I must admit it was not the shock of seeing me, nor Man On The Bush, he was a slight short spirit with a shock of red hair, that and his name were due to him trying to impress the first human he saw by trying to make it look as if he was rising out of a burning bush. Rather it was Preseli, a huge, grey almost rock like spirit who was so frightening to behold that even his own people cowered before him.

"Swear, all of you." His voice thundered. "Swear by The Maker Of All Things, swear by your ancestors. Swear you will have peace and no more shall die."

And so they all in turn swore and slowly departed each to their own people.

"Sunlight, stay." He said in a gentler voice. "Thank you for your belief. For too long we have been forgotten and without us these humans are a bit wayward. It is good to take on physical form, even if it is for a short time. My hope is that now they recognise me again I will have some influence over them. But you, Bush, you have instilled in your people a resentment far too long, who knows but in the future you may be known as Man On but I fear Bush will probably stick. It is not

Moonpool you should be angry with but your own love of pranks and your wanting to impress."

"I can tell you this Bush." Said Sunlight. "Moonpool will not be remembered in the distant ages, but you will, the town that will grow will always bear your name On a Bush in a language yet to come as Preseli suggested. This I have dreamed. I am sorry Moonpool."

"Let us at least make peace between us. We have had little to do with each other and I am afraid some of the blame must rest on us as a result." Said Preseli. "Maybe our peace will help our people have peace."

"Moonpool, accept my apology." Said Bush. "You have always been closer to your people than I to mine, you understand them better than I do, and perhaps I can learn something from this."

And with that they both left, leaving me alone with Sunlight.

"If I am not remembered what happens to me?" I asked.

Sunlight was silent in thought, perhaps regretting that she had let this slip.

"I do not know. You will have a choice and I cannot see which you chose."

Chapter 23

Plan

Some nights later I stood in the thin place and gazed up at the stars, there was no Moon in the sky that night for she has concerns far beyond my small valley. I was not alone, I am never really alone, but the peace and stability of the valley was my responsibility and I felt the weight of it, for even though as guardian and nature spirit it is the land I am responsible for, these people had chosen to settle here and therefore must come under my protection. One thing I had learned over the ages is that people are fickle, they frighten easily but they soon forget. I wanted to drink in being human for as long as I could and hoped that the peace between the peoples would last, if only there was a way I could influence them.

All the peoples had come together for the burning of the dead but mixed with their common grief was a tension and an underlying hatred and a great deal of anger. I know things change with time for humans but I have seen divisions go on over many generations even when people no longer know what the division is about. They needed something at this point to break down the rawness of the hatred.

If something wasn't done soon this hatred would simmer and threaten to erupt. The swearing of peace between the leaders would not hold for long because there was so much hatred and anger between all the people. There was also a resentment that their leaders had cosied up with each other and no retribution was exacted. Even though there was some distance between the camps it wasn't far enough and there was always the possibility that people from opposite sides could meet by chance or otherwise. There is always revenge which humans often mistake for justice.

Sunlight came and stood with me. We both stood and took in the night air in the relative peace of the place. I may not fully understand the human heart but there is within it a power greater than even they know.

"Wolfclaw has a daughter has he not?" I said.

"He has. Whitestar, she is growing fast and will soon be a woman." She looked at me and smiled a knowing smile.

"And Barwood has a son."

"Parlan, already he is a strong and wise young man, wiser than his father."

"You don't suppose?" I didn't need to say more.

"It would help. We must get them to meet somehow and see what happens. This would be a good match if we are successful."

"There will be opposition."

"In your experience when have alliances ever been easy?"

"In my experience I have found never to underestimate the power of love, but even I cannot force two people to love each other even though some of you people think I can."

An opportunity came fairly soon. Wolfclaw had gone with the recent trading party, they had a large quantity of leather and wool and it was getting difficult to carry everything, so they returned with one of those new carts drawn by a domesticated horse. There was much wonder and excitement among the three villages at the new arrival. Everyone wanted to see the horse and ask questions. Wolfclaw had to try and keep the people back because the horse was very nervous with so much attention and he was afraid she might hurt herself as she backed against the cart and was in danger of rearing up.

Since Wolfclaw had come to me to ask for help he was a very open person and it was easy for me to suggest that he take the horse and cart to see Barwood and offer its services for transporting things for trade to the Sea Port and to let him think it was his own idea. So I simply dropped the thought into his head.

"With the permission of the elders I will go over to Barwood and offer our services to transport trading goods for them." He said. "That way maybe we can keep the peace."

"Do you really want to help him after what he did?" Asked Greycloud, living up to his name as usual. "Why should we help him? Let him trade with the people of the Two Rivers."

"There is method in this, by using our horse and cart we can demand some form of payment from him, you know he owes us so much, we cannot lose. He can always say no but I can't see he'll get a better deal from the Two Rivers people."

After a short discussion among some of the older men Greycloud grudgingly gave his consent, seeing an opportunity to perhaps have some sort of payment for Barwood's attack.

I then planted a thought into Whitestar.

Whitestar, at that funny age when she is still only a child and not quite a woman, started jumping up and down. "Can I come?"

Wolfclaw could never say no to her, after the early death of Breeze he had to be both parents to her, the other women of the village were good but they were not her mother.

"Let me rest tonight at least, besides, the horse needs to rest as well. You can at least do this for me, Whitestar, look after the horse. I shall go in the morning and will consider this tonight."

Whitestar had ample time to help her father consider once she had rubbed down the horse and had fed her. So in the morning they set out together. It was quite a stiff climb out of the valley towards Bush so they walked with the horse and cart up the hill. Only on the top did they climb onto the cart and I could only follow them so far, relations between Bush and me were not good and I didn't think he would appreciate my entering his land. Therefore the rest I would have to leave to fate and whatever plan The Maker Of All Things had.

The next day the cart returned and, to my surprise and expectant hope, Parlan was with them. They had a large quantity of stone and wood.

"What is this then?" Asked Greycloud.

"This is building materials for Sea Port. It seems someone was listening the other day." Said Wolfclaw

"I can see that. What I want to know is what is he doing there? How dare he enter our valley."

"I asked him to come. Do not be surprised if no one fully trusts anyone, we have good reason to trust them in this instance because I have their goods already but they don't trust us yet, they suspected we would just take their goods. No argument, we stop here tonight and tomorrow load up some straw for roofing and take everything to Sea Port in the morning."

"And him?"

"Tonight he sleeps with us, that way I can be sure you won't be stabbing him in the night old man."

There was a great deal of grumbling in the night, Greycloud was not the only one who was far from happy, very few people were and discussions round the fire went late into the night. But Wolfclaw was held in high esteem and the appearance of three spirits still kept them wary at least for the moment. They were never sure how much I could hear and see. We who they refer to as gods and goddesses are a mystery to mortals. So, although there was much talk there was no action.

The night passed without incident. Wolfclaw made sure he slept between his daughter and the young man, he was a much more astute man than I had given him credit for, I believed he understood my plan and along with other plans of his own was helping it along.

The horse was hitched to the cart, the straw was added to the load and the cart rolled on. Wolfclaw and Parlan went with the cart while Whitestar, to her dismay and despite her continual pleading, was left in the camp. They walked as the horse could not pull the laden cart and them and certainly not on the rough track. It would take a day to get there, a day to trade and a day to return.

Greycloud, being Wolfclaw's uncle, was left in charge, though he was under the watchful eye of Sunlight and, he suspected, me. He was not a bad man and he was a good leader and the people got on with their daily lives and their usual tasks, again this was a very clever move by Wolfclaw. The daily tasks were made so much more difficult as so many people had been killed or badly injured, there were barely enough people to do all the work.

Whitestar was kept busy milking cows and helping making the cheese. But she still found time to fret and hardly slept the two nights they were away.

"You can forget about that son of a backstabbing weasel, once he goes back to his village he stays there and you stay here." Cautioned Greycloud. "I don't know what your father was thinking of, you are his only child and the responsibility of Village Ban will be yours after his days. Much as I wish my son Hawk to be leader it is not his place it is yours. Has Wolfclaw taught you nothing about responsibility? He has always been too soft on you, sometimes I fear for the future of the village."

"I don't know what you mean?"

"Don't know what I mean? I wasn't born yesterday, I saw you making doe eyes at that swine and I hear you sigh in the night. He and his people are still our sworn enemies. Besides, you are much too young to be thinking of such things."

"My mother was the same age as me."

"Yes, and she died in childbirth. And where would you live, he cannot live here quite apart from his being the next leader of his camp and you cannot live there, I cannot see them making you very welcome and by all accounts it is not a nice place to live."

"What is any of that to you? Besides I have only met him once."

"Once, remember that. There is bad blood between us, once will not wipe that out."

Chapter 24

Unrest

The second night Sunlight was standing in the thin place gazing up at the Moon, a new Moon that was always a sign of hope and humans like to wish on a new Moon and Silverwheel is always obliging if it is in her power. I didn't want to intrude on Sunlight but she was so deeply troubled I felt compelled to stand by her.

"What is it?" I asked.

"I know there is a deep anger and hatred, it seems our plans for Whitestar and Parlan seem to be working out but there will be so much opposition. Greycloud, although the most vocal, is probably the least of our worries, after all he must see an opportunity for his son. It is always the people who don't say anything that you have to watch out for."

"These are going to be difficult days for sure, but you humans do have a way of working these things out. The passing of time is a useful gift to you on occasions like this."

She was silent for a time, and then shook her head. "No. It's more than just the people, I can feel it. Every time I come down here from the village I feel such darkness until I come here, there is always peace here."

"The darkness, where do you feel it the most?"

"I feel it whenever I pass the site where the dead were burned."

From Sunlight's perspective I didn't move merely paused in thought. I was at the site of the burning and back again in a twinkling that she was not aware of, the ground was still blackened and I could still hear the sound of fighting. I felt a presence, or rather many presences, some of those who had died had not passed over. It was as if the fight went on for them.

"I have known this to happen at times with humans." I said to Sunlight. "I do not understand fully what happens to you when you die but your spirit lives on and passes into the Otherworld. Sometimes your spirit does not move on but hangs on to this world for so many different reasons. Over many generations the spirit gets tired of holding on and fades into the Otherworld since no one they know is left and no one remembers them so they lose their grasp. But this is different, for many of the spirits that are holding on to this world are doing so out of hatred for each other, it was a mistake to burn them together."

"What can we do?"

"I must ask The Maker Of All Things. Only he knows."

"Will he appear? Can I ask him?"

"You can ask him but he will not appear, even I have not seen him and I have been since before this world."

"How do I ask him then if I cannot see him?"

"Talk to him in your spirit."

This we both did.

"O Maker Of All Things, how can we help the dead of the battle who do not move on?" I asked.

There was silence for a moment.

"I do not interfere with the free will of people." He said. "I do not force them to move on. I send my messengers among them so they can be guided but I will not do more than that."

"But there is an evil that surrounds the site and it is affecting everyone in the area, surely those who still live have a right to peace."

He said no more to me.

"Anything?" Sunlight asked.

"No, nothing, perhaps this is between you and him."

"Then what do we do now?"

"We hold vigil, we wait."

So we waited all that night in silence.

As morning approached he must have spoken to Sunlight because she stood and picked up a bowl from the stone that still lay in the thin place. She walked out of the enclosure and over to the river and filled the bowl with water. She brought it back to the stone and placed it on top.

"O Maker Of All Things." She said, holding her hands over the bowl. "Make this water holy, fill it with peace."

She picked it up and raised it to the Sun for a moment as it rose over the brow of the hill.

"Come, Moonpool."

She led me up the track to the sight of the burning. Taking a sprig of oak from her belt she repeatedly dipped the sprig in the water and sprayed it over the site.

"Give peace to the souls who remain, may they pass over and be at rest. You who fight on, for you the fight is over now and no one has won, you need to rest now and leave the future to the living. This I command in the name of The Maker Of All Things."

She continued to spray the water.

"Turn to the light, lay down your hatred and be at peace."

Some of the souls turned to see the messengers and I could feel the hatred and anger ease considerably, but it did not go away completely for hatred runs so deeply.

"I believe this is the best we can do Moonpool." She sighed. "There will always be those who hang on and refuse to see."

Certainly things were somewhat better in the village, the very air seemed lighter. Though there was now a stain of anger on the land and I felt it deep within me. I had to trust that this would fade in time.

Wolfclaw and Parlan returned later that day, the cart was laden with cloth and ale and wine and a few trinkets of bronze and a strange packet for Sunlight. There was some excitement among the people, for this was the largest trade that had been done because the cart could carry so much. After discussion and much bartering both sides eventually agreed what Parlan should take back to his people. All the items that were being kept were unloaded then Wolfclaw asked Greycloud to go with Parlan to take the horse and cart over in his place. Greycloud was surprised to be asked, he was not happy about it but agreed to do so.

"Can I go?" Begged Whitestar.

"No." Said her father firmly. "You have work here."

"How did it go with Parlan?"

Wolfclaw didn't answer. He gave instruction to Greycloud about the care of the horse and how to handle the cart. Then he wished them a safe journey and sent them on their way. Wolfclaw was a very astute man and he knew Greycloud would have to stay the night and hoped Barwood would look after him well. This was a risk, but if there was to be peace it had to be tried.

Chapter 25

Healing

Early the next morning just before the Sun broke over the hill Sunlight was in the thin place, the sky was a deep and dark blue becoming gradually lighter and a gentle breeze blew along the valley from the east. She stood for some time in front of the stone in silence. Then slowly and carefully she placed a fired clay disc on the altar that she had asked to be specially made in Pole's Camp, she placed some smouldering wood on the disc and placed a few pieces of something from the strange packet on the wood. The substance began to burn and give off a fragrant smoke.

"I burn this myrrh to ward off the evil that has come to this valley and to Moonpool. It is also a gift to Moonpool and an apology for my demands on her." She said softly. "She has watched over us and we have not always respected her yet we owe everything to her and the abundance of her valley."

As the Sun broke over the horizon she knelt for a moment then slowly walked away, turning back briefly and bowing low as she left the area then slowly walked back up to the village.

Only after she had gone far enough did I take on human form and breathed in the aromatic smoke.

It did calm the deep anger somewhat, in my human form I was touched by her concern and that more than anything helped me. The attack and the killing would be a scar in the valley for a long time but it was less raw now. I only hoped that the people of the valley would feel this too and much of the anger would abate.

Greycloud returned with the empty cart before the sun had risen to its highest, but he was not empty handed. He was very quiet and thoughtful, it seemed much of his anger and resentment has subsided as well.

"How was it Greycloud?" Asked Wolfclaw. "Did they treat you well?"

"I will admit that Barwood was a good host, and he gave me this." He showed everyone a short bronze knife. "This does not make things right, he cannot bring back our dead but at least he is serious about peace. I could see Parlan's hand in this, what did you talk to him about on your visit to Sea Port?"

I have said before how astute Wolfclaw was, I could see his hand in this all the way through. But all he said was, "Parlan will be leader after his father, I trust he will be a wiser leader, and I just offered him advice."

Greycloud looked askance at him but no more was said.

Then Wolfclaw turned to his daughter. "Whitestar, could you go to Vellon's camp, they need help with the sheep, they lost many good people."

Whitestar was more than willing, she knew that Vellon's camp was much nearer Bush and the chances of seeing Parlan were much greater there, especially as sheep tend to wander a lot even without help.

It took the passing of another four seasons but Whitestar was following the flock over the hills just beyond my valley when she came across Parlan cutting down trees to clear more land for grazing cattle. I wasn't witness to their meeting but it was obvious from what happened as a result that the time they spent apart hadn't lessened their feelings for each other. She brought the sheep back then came straight down to her father to tell him of their intention.

Because they had waited both peoples were somewhat willing to accept the bond between them, there was still some grumbling but Greycloud at least was glad for he saw an opportunity for his son and his opinion carried so much weight. They came to my thin place for the ceremony of union at midsummer as the Sun was rising. Sunlight was beaming all over her face as she performed the ceremony. People came from all the villages including Bush's, it was a beautiful occasion and there was feasting and drinking afterwards. Not all hatred was put away, the hurt was still far too deep and too raw, but there would be no reason to fight even though there was no mixing of the peoples and there was still a lot of tension.

Whitestar went with Parlan to his people where he eventually became a much wiser leader than his father for he went out of his way to form better relations with the people of my valley. To Greycloud's pleasure although he would never admit it Hawk followed Wolfclaw and took a partner, Mountaindew, from among the people of the mountain, this was a surprise to everyone including me but again it helped heal divisions. A trade route was established between all the peoples and Sea Port which was growing steadily so that a second horse and cart were obtained and the valley prospered.

Sunlight, now old and grey was sitting on the hill that so long ago I had sat with Ban and she gazed over the whole valley.

"Moonpool." She said.

"Sunlight." I said, sitting beside her.

"We have done our best haven't we?"

"We have done well, considering everything we have done very well indeed. It is good that there are some wise heads among your people."

"I am old and there is no one suitable to follow me. Hawks brother Stag has been a reasonable student and is a capable holy man but I don't like the fact that he won't consult you."

I remembered when I first knew her and we danced in the holy place, how young I felt then. There was still a youth about her and I still felt young.

"He will find his own way. Hawk is wise enough for the two of them and he will often come to the thin place and talk. Do not fear, your people will survive and continue to prosper."

Chapter 26

Rebuilding

Hawk stood outside the thin place, watching from afar as Stag went through the rituals of Sunlights funeral with the people of the villages. The Sun was setting and her spirit was sent into the Otherworld in the west, the Sun blazed brightly for a moment on the horizon then was gone and the darkness slowly began to descend, soon the stars would appear. Hawk stood with his son Stallion who seemed more interested in the river.

"What is it Stallion? What do you see? Is it the fish?"

"I hear weeping."

Weeping, I hadn't realised I was. I was not in physical form and yet I was weeping. I was not always close to the humans but occasionally I do let myself get too close to someone. It is then I realise the vast chasm between me and them, their mortality means they come and go while I remain. I have my own kind but there is a closeness the humans have that I almost envy, this is probably because they have to fit all their lives, all their experiences, all their hopes and dreams into so short a time.

"Weeping?" Asked Hawk. "I don't hear anything."

"She has stopped now, she is very lonely."

"Who is?"

"The woman I cannot see."

"I wonder ..."

The next evening when all the work was done and everyone was settling down for the night and the Sun sank below the horizon again Hawk and Stallion returned and stood where they had before.

"Moonpool." Called Hawk.

I was reticent to appear. Sunlight because of her level of belief had all but made me appear when she wanted, although I was glad to do so having not been able to for so long. I don't believe she intended it that way but there is a thin line between request and demand. I was also shocked to realise that I had been weeping when not in physical form that I was afraid of my feelings if I had a human heart just then. And this was quite apart from having to admit to having certain feelings to humans. We spirits do tend to be somewhat proud and a little superior at times.

"Who is Moonpool?" Asked Stallion.

"She is our goddess, she is good and kind and has always looked after our ancestors in this valley."

"Always?"

"Always, she was here when Ban first came."

"She must be really old."

This tickled me so much that I could resist no longer and I stood beside them. But the emotion of the loss of Sunlight was hard to bear as it hit me the moment I took on human form. She had made me feel so young right up until the end and she of all the humans I have met treated me most as an equal even though she knew full well we were not.

"You are not old." Said Stallion looking up at me.

"Stallion!" Said his father sharply. He then knelt, pulling his son down too. "Moonpool, may I present to you Stallion, my son. He will be leader after me so I ask you to bless him and look over him."

It was a while before I could speak, they patiently waited because they could not possibly rush me, unaware of my inner turmoil.

"Hawk." I said at last. "You have been a wise leader and I see in Stallion's heart he will be too. He is a gentle soul and your people will love him. Now, stand on your feet."

They did not stand but waited, I lay my hand on Stallion's head for a moment. He was a very open person and I could tell he was indeed a wise and kind person. But the emotions welled up inside, too much to bear, and I was gone.

While one of the carts was being taken into the mountains the other cart took pots, cheeses, dried meats and straw to Sea Port, the two people with it also drove a couple of young heifers with them. A day later they returned, the cart itself was empty but four men and a woman and four horses returned with it. These newcomers had swarthy complexions and said they had come from a distant land across the sea, their knowledge of the local language was very patchy but they were able to make themselves understood well enough. One of the men and the woman were excellent horse handlers, the other men had heard rumour that our valley had more women than men and needed help to rebuild and with the heavy tasks, and what was left unsaid possibly partners for the women too. Of course this was all true and they were made very welcome indeed, they were a new race to the people and everyone wanted to know about the land they were from. It was a land that didn't get so dark and cold during the winter months, where the Sun was fierce and higher in the sky.

Stallion took to the two horse handlers and the horses, his was such a gentle soul that the horses that were naturally skittish creatures, took to him too and he soon learned all about them. He had a way of holding their heads down to himself, talking close to them and calming them, then getting them to do whatever he asked.

Many of the round houses of the three villages were rebuilt at this time thanks to the extra hands. Also the ditch of the thin place was re-dug and the bank repaired. It also meant that people could be spared to drive sheep and cattle into Sea Port because live animals were much better for trade.

Stallion, Saron and Wenda kept the horses on the hills to the north, all around the hill where I once sat with Ban. Sometimes Stallion would sit there and gaze across the valley. I felt he would be glad of my company but he would never impose or demand. So once in a while I would sit with him.

"Things are picking up for us aren't they?" He said. "There is an air of peace over the valley."

I looked at him, his gaze was far away.

"This is generally a peaceful valley, as long as your people are left alone." I said.

"Surely we are your people. You are our goddess."

"I prefer spirit of the valley."

"If you are the spirit of the valley why are you called Moonpool then?"

"Once, much of this valley was filled with a lake. When your ancestor Ban first saw the lake it was in the night, he saw the Moon reflected in it and when he saw me he named me Moonpool and that is who I am ever since."

"What happened to the lake?"

I found him such an easy person to talk to that it was a relief to tell a human about some of my grief. While we talked I looked across the valley and I could see the areas where the trees had been cut down to make room for grazing. Dotted about where huts people had put up to be near their animals. Slowly the land was being tamed and filled.

"When I was young I heard you crying. You are very sad aren't you?" He said.

"Too many people have come and gone. I sometimes think I should not have got involved so much with your people. Most of my kin stay quite remote while some, like Little Rainbow, have got too close to someone and have become human."

He sat and thought about this.

"Would you ever become human?"

I sighed deeply. He had hit on my deep yearning which I had been unwilling to face.

"I don't know, Stallion, I just don't know. I do worry what would happen to my valley, would it be empty or would another spirit replace me? I know that good rarely comes of a spirit becoming human."

I looked at him, wondering if there was something else behind the question. He was such an open person and there was nothing else behind the question, it was just innocent curiosity. I was amazed that I spoke to him of things I had shared with no one else and I was concerned that I had given too much away. But there was no malice in him and I knew without a doubt that this would end with him.

"Is there not someone you can ask?" He said at last.

"Silverwheel is very wise but she doesn't know the future any more than I do. I have asked The Maker Of All Things but he says that all his creatures have to make their own way and it is not for us to know the future. I have found that you humans sometimes get a glimpse but a glimpse is all it is."

Again we sat in silence for some time.

"There is peace now." He said after a while. "But the world is changing."

"Yes, there is peace here for now. You must always be vigilant Stallion. You know I will do what I can but I am spirit of the valley and have no say over the wills of people."

Chapter 27

Chieftain

Snow, the young holy woman from Vellon's people, stood by the altar and waited in silence, gazing down the valley at the river winding through, a mist hung still in the valley and the Sun was slowly burning it away, it promised to be a very fine day. Stag had taught her what he knew but Stallion and I had taught her much as well, so she was a very good and wise holy woman. Some myrrh was burning steadily on the altar before the pot with Hawks ashes. There was a finely woven cloak and a decorated bronze clasp that had been laid out on the altar.

Stallion was leading the people down the track from the village and he stopped at the entrance to the site.

"I am Stallion, son of Hawk." He announced. "As I am bidden I have come to ask the people of the three camps to accept me as Chieftain."

"Enter, Stallion." Snow replied turning to face him. "Enter the sanctuary with the people and receive the mantle."

He entered and the people followed behind.

"Do you, the people of the three camps wish Stallion to be your Chieftain?" She called out.

"The people of Ban wish Stallion to be Chieftain. We are one people."

"The people of Pole wish Stallion to be Chieftain. We are one people."

"The people of Vellon wish Stallion to be Chieftain. We are one people."

"Stallion, do you accept the call of all people to be Chieftain?"

"I accept."

Snow got to her knees and Stallion followed.

"If Moonpool is willing I humbly beg her blessing." Said Stallion.

How could I possibly refuse this request? I stood beside Snow. A collective gasp arose from all the people, I don't just appear in front of people like that normally and certainly not often to so many and I forget the surprise it causes.

"Stallion." I said laying my hand on his shoulder. "You have already proved yourself a wise and kind man, liked by everyone, and I know you will lead our people well. You have my blessing."

Snow and Stallion stood. Snow took the pot of Hawk's ashes and handed them to Stallion.

"Give your father to the land, place him with Ban."

He took the pot, going round the altar to the part of the bank where Ban's bones were. There he poured the ashes out onto the bank and as they fell they almost glowed in the light of the sun.

"Rest with our ancestors, father, you have earned your place with them."

The people cheered, Hawk was a popular leader and though not officially leader of all the people until this moment his guidance was always sought and his wisdom relied upon.

Stallion broke the pot and left the pieces on top of the bank then returned to stand before Snow.

Snow picked up the cloak and placed it on him. Then she took the broach and handed it to me. I pinned it to the edges of the cloak, fastening it together across his chest. His head was bowed and he felt deeply the honour of this act.

Turning to the people he declared. "You have appointed me your Chieftain and I will do my best to lead you all with wisdom and justice. Remember this, the position we have created this day need not be hereditary. Each Chieftain must be chosen by you, it is an honour and not a right."

He bowed to me, then to Snow and then to the people.

"A feast is prepared." He called out. "Let us celebrate."

With shouts and cheers the people left the sanctuary, picking Stallion up and carrying him on their shoulders they trooped back to Village Ban singing.

"Do you eat and drink?" Snow asked me when all the people had gone and the sanctuary had become quiet. "I never thought to ask before. Come with us and share the feast."

I smiled. "I have never tried, I certainly don't need to. Thank you but I don't think it would be a good idea. This is a time for your people not me."

The invitation had been kindly meant and the temptation was great but on many levels I needed to keep my distance.

Stallion was a good leader. He would come to the sanctuary to settle disputes, which were not many. Through trade he acquired a longer bronze sword and shield because he knew that there was always a threat from other tribes, not necessarily the close ones as before, with them the peace still held and it may be that they would all need to fight together, but the world was becoming a busier place and there were men who wished for power over greater areas. For this reason other bronze weapons were traded for and the men were taught to use them, the hunter had now been replaced by the warrior.

When Stallion and Wildflower from Sea Port came together one spring Snow performed the ceremony in the sanctuary. The place was adorned with wild flowers and blossoms. Snow did request my presence but I needed to let the humans get on with their lives and develop without interference. I hoped that she understood this, I knew Stallion would.

Soon a son was born to them, Stallion named him Raven on account of his thick black hair when he was born.

Chapter 28

Raid

As Raven grew he followed his father with horses, he had a natural affinity with them. They were so calm with him he could train them to be ridden and he soon had a band of men and women who were excellent riders.

He brought his favourite horse to the river and stood gazing at the swirling current for some time. The horse stood patiently beside him and he did not move for a long time apart from patting the horse every now and then.

"Moonpool." He called.

Sometimes I do not wish to be at someone's beck and call.

He took a bronze pin from his cloak and threw it suddenly into the river. Then he knelt down.

"My apologies Moonpool, in my excitement I forgot my manners."

"Apology accepted." I said as I stood before him.

The horse began to nuzzle my hand, so I patted him, lifted his head and looked into his eyes. Horses are quite intelligent and very open. I spoke to his mind of courage, something I felt he needed and humans do not always understand them.

"Raven, you can stand now."

Reluctantly he stood but kept his eyes lowered.

"Moonpool, I hope you don't mind but I named this horse after you, yes I know he is a stallion but he is very calm and wise and strong like you."

"Flatterer. But call him that if you wish. I suppose you want my blessing on him?"

"If you please."

"Already done."

"Raven! Raven!" A slim man was running down the track, sweat pouring off him and his legs beginning to buckle under him.

"Yren!" Raven ran to meet him. "What is it? Raiders?"

"Yes, come quick, we have seen the warning fires and they are on their way." With that his legs gave way under him and Raven was just quick enough to catch him.

"Moonpool, can I impose on you to look after him? I must go to Sea Port for my mother's father must have sent him."

I took hold of Yren while Raven grabbed a horn from his belt and blew three short blasts. Then he jumped on his horse and headed to the village. There he met with his band of riders, was handed his father's bronze sword, the others already having theirs, they all mounted and off they rode. In human form I could not watch them going, I had to half support Yren back to the village, I could have carried him but he insisted he could walk.

Fortunately Snow was there waiting, she took him into the large house and lay him on a bed.

"He's from Sea Port isn't he?" She asked.

"Yes, there is going to be a raid there and Raven has taken his band of riders to help."

I couldn't help noticing how old Snow was getting. I was glad to see Raven's sister's daughter Starbright in attendance, Snow had chosen a worthy successor.

The two were intent on their patient so I took the opportunity to find out where Raven and the others were, with the permission of my brothers of course. Raven and his band were already half way to Sea Port where I could see the raiders drawing up in their boats, a hail of arrows passing back and forth between them and the people of the town. The tidal river was almost black with the number of boats and despite their losses they gained the land and began charging the gates of the fort. They brought combustible materials with them and soon the gate was set alight. The smoke made it difficult for the defenders to see but the raiders had withdrawn slightly waiting for the gate to fall. This gave Raven and his band enough time to come up behind the raiders so when the gate began to fall away they were caught between the townspeople with swords and spears before them and the swift assault of fighters on horseback behind.

Raven and his band were excellent riders and their practice with swords while on horseback paid off. They tore into the raiders whose surprise was so great not one of our people was hurt. Raven's horse Moonpool courageously led them right up to the gate and the defending townspeople. Seeing the devastating effect of mounted warriors on the attackers gave them added courage and as Raven turned his horse he led them out into the thick of the fighting dividing the attackers into two groups weakening them both. Cut off from half of his forces wisely the leader of the raiders blew three blasts on his horn and they all threw down their arms and begged for mercy, the raid over as quickly as it had begun.

The town safe and our people unhurt I returned. "How is Yren?" I asked.

"Just exhausted. He will recover soon enough. He must have run all the way." Said Snow. "It is Raven and the others I am worried about."

"Raven and the others are fine. They got there just as the raiders were breaking through the gate so they were caught in the middle and it wasn't long before they lay down their arms. Many of the townspeople are killed or injured and the raiders have suffered heavy losses but none of our people were hurt."

Snow looked at me with relief and surprise. "Of course you know this, sorry if I doubt you."

Raven and the others stayed a few days, they were heroes who saved the town, now called Sea Fort because of the need for protection, this would not be the last raid but hopefully the enemy would be more wary after news of this got back. The people of Sea Fort had learned of their weakness and had plans to build greater defences. Immediately they began work on increasing the fortifications of the town. As was their right the townspeople demanded a high price for sparing the lives of the raiders and this included the life of their leader and forced labour for most of the others. A few they allowed to return so that the news of their defeat would be passed back. From the spoil they presented Raven with a gold cloak pin among many other items of value for his band.

When Raven and his warriors returned there was great excitement, a feast was prepared on the flat land behind the holy place and they celebrated through the night. Stallion was so proud of his son.

"Is there any doubt." He shouted in the midst of the revelry. "My son will be Cheiftain after me."

Cheers.

He lifted his hand for silence. "But we must still decide as a people and not because I say it, I promised this would not be a position passed down through families and I will abide by this promise and if you choose someone else I will abide by your decision. Therefore I ask you all, are you all in favour?"

"Camp Ban are in favour."

"Camp Pole are in favour."

"Camp Vellon are in favour."

Cheers again from all the people.

"Is there anyone else you would have lead you?"

Silence.

"But be warned. We live in dangerous times, there are threats from all sides, we need to have friends and make alliances. Ours is a good land and others will look upon it with greedy eyes, we must be prepared. You have proved yourself now but it will not always be so easy."

"We are ready." Many of them shouted. "Raven will lead us."

Despite this Stallion looked sad. The world was changing and peace could no longer be taken for granted. The celebrations continued but there was an underlying sense of unease among many of the people.

Chapter 29

Fears

Starbright often came to the sanctuary in the night simply to stand and watch and think, to watch the stars change with the seasons when the sky was clear, to watch the Moon wax and wane. She had grown to be a wise and far seeing woman, a very capable holy woman and healer of the sick after Snow passed into the west. Raven very sensibly consulted her all the time after his father also died and between them they brought stability and peace to the valley. Rumours of fighting came from afar but all was quiet here.

I let them be.

People still occasionally brought small gifts to toss into the river, asking for good weather, a kind and loving partner, health for a relative. Any item thrown into the river with a wish for a curse strangely got washed straight back onto the bank so this didn't happen often and was never repeated.

On one return trip from Bush the traders brought news that a band of raiders from a land across the sea to the west had landed on the far coast. They were a fierce people and had completely overrun the people who lived by the sea. It was feared that they wouldn't stop there since they had come across the sea for the sole purpose of conquest.

The next morning Raven came to the sanctuary with Starbright. Raven brought a bowl with slowly burning charcoal, placed it on the altar and Starbright dropped in some basil, dill, rosemary and wild garlic.

"Moonpool, protect us from attack, let us live here in peace." She said.

"This is your land and you have been good to us over the generations. We come to you again for aid. If the raiders come here can you help us defend your valley for in time they surely will." Raven added.

"O Maker f All Things." Said Starbright. "We ask nothing more than you allow us to remain here and keep our little ones safe."

Raven sank to his knees, there was a question, or perhaps a decision and he didn't know which way to go.

"Moonpool." He said at last. "I answered the call from Sea Port to help defend their town, I have not been called to this fight so have I the right to go and even if I did would I succeed. By all accounts the invaders have gained a foothold on the land and are by now well defended. What should I do? If I do nothing they will grow stronger, more will come across the sea and then how can we stand against them?"

I cannot foresee the future and I do not understand The Maker Of All Things' plan. I could not advise him. Much as I wanted to be there with him there would be no point, this was something he had to decide for himself. Sometimes I interfere too much, the humans must be allowed to make their own way in the world.

In the depths of the night when no one was about and the Moon was full I sat on Ban's bank with Silverwheel.

"What is wrong with these humans that they want to fight and take what someone else has?" I asked.

"We are no better Moonpool, even many of the messengers went against The Maker Of All Things and some of them still roam about causing trouble. You are a peaceful spirit and although you have seen much you should be grateful you have not seen what I see. It will come, even to your valley, I say this not because I know the future any more than you rather I know human nature. These humans multiply so quickly, they make new things, they change and adapt. There is not another creature in the world like them. They also fight for so many reasons even I can't keep up with them and they excel at making newer weapons."

Much of this I knew but it was still frightening to have it spelled out.

"Although you are a peaceful spirit, Moonpool, as these people have asked then it is not interfering if you do help them. There may come a time when they believe they do not need you or The Maker Of All Things, it cannot harm if you encourage their faith in powers greater than themselves for the time being. However, be assured the raiders are a long way off and many peoples stand between you and them. They may not come this far but who can tell. As the Moon moves west I must speak to the spirit of the peninsular who is mourning the loss of many good people."

"Why are you so sad?" Starbright asked.

I looked up at the Moon. I listened to the stars. I had been so wrapped in my own thoughts I hadn't noticed her approach. I turned to her.

"I mourn the loss of many people on the far coast, the cruelty and the greed of some humans saddens me, it is for no reason that they attack and kill."

"We are not all bad."

"No. Whatever happens this I know, although humans have potential for so much cruelty and evil it is only a small number, most of you are good and kind, often better than you think yourselves to be."

"You know everything, Moonpool, are we in danger."

"For now the raiders are a long way off and many people and spirits stand in their way. And if they should get this far then put your trust in Raven. He is a good fighter and a good leader and I have some powers that you know nothing of."

"I fear for Raven. I fear that he will want to go and face the enemy before they get any further. What is worse is that he is right, it is better that he face them while they are still few than wait for their numbers to grow and march across all the lands to get here."

"Again I say trust Raven. If he does decide to go it will because he has thought everything through and has reasoned that if he acts soon he has a good chance of prevailing."

"What if he is wrong? What if the enemy is too strong? What if he is killed?"

"I am sure he has thought of that too."

We were both silent for a while.

"How did you know to find me here?" I asked.

"I saw something glowing on the hill and came to see what it was but it is gone."

"That was Silverwheel, it is natural for her to shine."

"Silverwheel?" She was shocked for a moment to think that she had come down from the Moon and been on this hill. "Then can she help?"

"It is not her place, the whole world is a concern to her but I am sure she would support me if necessary."

Chapter 30

Battle

The news that conflict was on its way even though still a long way off quickly spread through the villages. Raven came to the river and tossed a bronze clasp in, the water swirled around and over it and it sank into the depths. Then he entered the sanctuary. For some time he just stood, deep in thought, it was an overcast day and there were a few drops of rain but they didn't amount to much. I knew what he wanted and I waited. How often now have I waited, I can wait for ever but the humans cannot and at times I feel myself caught up in the time that sometimes drags for them even when not in physical form.

"Moonpool. I intend to take a few warriors with me to offer some help to the people in the west, we need allies and so do they. I hope it will not come to a fight, who knows but it might be enough to stand with them to show the invaders they can come no further. We must all stand together in this land. All I ask is your blessing."

I cannot protect him outside the valley so I wasn't sure what blessing he thought I could give. When one human gives a blessing to another it is simply permission or a hope for protection, I could easily do that but the fact that he was asking me probably meant that he reckoned I could do more. I waited.

"Please do not tell Starbright. I will tell her we are just riding over to Bush for a conference."

Then he left without waiting for any response from me.

Early the next morning he left with five and one other horse warriors. As far as anyone knew they went to a conference with the people of Bush village. If Starbright suspected anything she didn't show it. Of course his first call was with the people of Bush but it didn't stop there. He had not lied but it was not all the truth for he did hold a conference with them. There was a discussion, he suggested they band together and perhaps others along the way would join and they were willing to follow his lead. I knew where he was going so as they went from village to village and with the permission of the local spirits, and in company with them I followed Raven and a growing number of people who went with him from each village. Everywhere people were waiting for a leader decisive enough to do something rather than wait and be picked off one by one, and Raven was that man. Such was his force of personality they followed whatever may befall.

The Sun rose and set twice by the time we arrived at the coast. Raven had a sizeable army, mostly on foot, not every village had riding horses though the last town they passed through were well trained on horseback. We came to the invaders camp, Raven's force outnumbered the enemy but they were dug in and defending and would be difficult to displace. We also outnumbered the Tuatha de Dannan who had come with them but only just, and they are fierce spirits and used to fighting while we are not.

Raven rode towards the camp alone.

"I am Raven of the Valley of Moonpool and I have come with all the tribes of the peninsula firstly to ask why you have come and have declared war on us and killed innocent people, and secondly to demand that you leave and never return."

A large bear of a man in full bronze armour stood at the gate.

"I am Oengus across the sea. I take what I will and who is there to stop me."

"We are here to stop you, you see all the fighters I have with me? There are more behind."

"Ha, and there are more behind me too. You have no idea how vast the land is that I come from and we are all fighters."

"You refuse to leave then?"

"Why? I see no reason."

"Is that your final word?"

"It is my only word." And with that he lifted his spear and hurled it at Raven.

That was his mistake. He had started the conflict before his people were ready.

Because of a subtle deflection that even I didn't notice where it came from it missed. Raven charged at him and his army followed. With Oengus in the gate perhaps Raven could get there before the gate was shut. There was a hail of arrows on both sides but because of the suddenness of the attack Raven's troops gained the gate before many found their mark. Raven cut down Oengus even as he lifted his sword to defend himself, a blow aimed at his head was deflected but it still bit deep into his shoulder where there was only a leather strap, obviously his armour was not designed to protect from a foe on horseback.

I concentrated on protecting Raven and giving his sword arm extra strength so I missed what was happening behind. I had to contend with one of their spirits all the time who was determined to have Raven killed, anger and rage may be powerful in battle but it blinds to the subtlety of tactics and the agility of a smaller spirit, also I surprised him, he didn't expect such a fight on his hands. As a result Raven drove far into the camp, his sword flashing right and left. He drove on almost to the sea then wheeled round. His mounted fighters had followed him into the camp and had cut right through the centre.

He saw many of his people had been killed but the invaders had suffered far worse. Many of the houses had somehow spontaneously burst into flame and I guessed Bush had been at work. Because many of the riders had entered the fort so suddenly the gate could not be closed and most of the foot warriors had gained the gate and were fighting with sword and knife and club. For all the aggression of the enemy these were people defending their homes and loved ones behind them and fought with a determination that surprised the foe. Oengus hadn't been killed but his right arm was useless and he was struggling to his feet with his sword in his left hand. The mounted warriors surrounded him and Raven called out.

"And what word have you now Oengus across the sea?"

Without the use of his right arm, his camp in flames, his force severely depleted and his spirits caught off guard by the unexpected tactics and ferocity of the local spirits he had no option but to throw down his sword and fall to his knees, raising his left arm above his head in surrender.

Slowly the fighting abated, the foreign spirits retreated to the edge of the sea and all the invaders threw down their swords and their axes and their clubs. A cheer went up from Raven's troop with much clashing of spears and swords on shields. None of us were visible throughout all this, let the humans believe it was their victory and it was enough for us to be proud of our people.

Chapter 31

Unity

Starbright was frantically pacing up and down the sanctuary. She paid no heed to the driving rain for she could not just stand and wait. She knew where Raven had gone, even if she had not suspected it in the beginning he had been away so long now it was obvious. I guessed she had been doing this for days calling out to me but I had not been here.

"Moonpool, Moonpool, please I beg you. Give me a sign, anything."

Sun or rain is all the same to me, the land needs them both and I find it quite refreshing to be rained on in human form, especially now, especially after so much bloodshed. So I stood in front of her as she paced.

"Starbright, all is well, Raven is safe."

"Oh."

The words 'where have you been' died on her lips which was just as well, you don't say that sort of thing to your goddess. She quickly realised where I had been, she must have guessed I would have been with Raven and the others when they didn't come back.

"Oh." She said again. This time with relief.

She stopped her pacing and realised it was raining.

"Oh." She said a third time. "Can we talk somewhere dry."

I was a bit put out by what she nearly said since I am not after all at her beck and call.

"You talk somewhere dry if you wish, I am going to enjoy the rain." And I lifted my face to the rain and let it wash over me.

"You went with them? What happened?"

"Raven will tell you when he gets back. Go and get dry, I really do need to soak up the rain."

This was true. I needed to cool down. I am not a violent spirit, though I will defend the valley, and Raven as good as asked for my help so I went with him. People died even though it was justified, nature can be cruel and I see death all the time yet somehow this felt different. As the humans increased the world changed and we seem to be carried along with that change. Change is part of the universe but not as rapid as with the humans. I began to feel I wanted to stop at that point. The rain was cool and refreshing but could it wash away all the blood that I helped to shed?

The Earth turned on its axis and my valley passed under the Sun many more times before Raven returned. And on a bright and clear day he returned to cheers and shouts, some of those he had gone with never returned but many strangers from different villages to the west returned with him shouting out.

"People of Moonpool Valley rejoice and welcome Raven, Chieftain of the West.

"What does this mean?" Starlight shouted up to Raven over the roar of many voices.

Raven was wearing a new cloak, fastened with a golden broach and he carried a very ornate bronze shield.

"I have been appointed Chieftain of all the villages from here westward to the coast. We have unity between all the people. Tonight we celebrate."

Cheers everywhere and all the people began chanting his name.

"And where is Moonpool? Without her we may not have fared so well, the gods of the enemy were fierce but she led our gods to hold them at bay."

"I have not seen her for days." Said Starlight lowering her face. "I might have angered her."

She had not angered me but it might be as well to let her think so.

"Why do you think that?"

"I nearly asked her where she had been when I had been calling her for days."

"You didn't."

"Very nearly, but you never know how much she knows, she is a goddess after all, she probably knows I was thinking it."

Raven didn't have a chance to answer as they were separated by the throng of people and he was lifted off his horse and carried along to the celebrations.

At the height of the celebrations that night Raven slipped away and came to the temple. There he placed his second old bronze clasp on the altar.

"Moonpool. I know how you helped me personally, I could not see you but I felt your protective presence and your strength in my arm, I have no idea what it cost you to do so. I don't know when you left but you need to know that it did not end badly. We did not kill Oengus nor did we send him and his people back. He owes us much and we made an agreement with him. He and his people will serve us and they will be our first defence against the next invaders, after all by sparing their lives now they will be the first to lose them later if we are attacked again and don't worry there are enough people to keep an eye on him. I am Chieftain of the west and may be called on again to defend the peninsular; I cannot expect you to protect me like that again but thank you again for your help this time. Accept this small token from me."

Rather than appear to him I caused a jackdaw to swoop down and pick up the offering, showing that I accepted it and his words. And the jackdaw was very grateful.

He knelt at the altar for a moment. "And forgive Starlight for her thoughts, we humans cannot see things from your perspective and there is so much we worry about and are frightened of."

He stood for a moment before leaving.

"I also understand your need to be alone." And he left.

He was right, I needed some space.

Chapter 32

Identity

I stood where I had stood behind Ban when first I saw a human and took on human form. It was deepest night again and the Moon was full. There was no lake now and no reflection of the Moon, the land had changed, there were fields now and hedges keeping the cattle from roaming and small huts built so those looking after the cattle could live near them. The humans had made their mark and had tamed the land.

So who am I? I was only Moonpool because Ban saw the Moon's reflection in the lake and he was dreaming and spoke his thoughts out loud. Until then I just was. Much of who I am now seems to be who the humans expected me to be. I felt they had tamed me as much as they had tamed the land.

"Oh Maker Of All Things. Who am I?"

He remained silent. Obviously it was one of those mysteries we are not supposed to know.

"You are Moonpool." Said a voice behind me.

"Moonpool?" I answered as Starlight drew alongside me. "And who or what is Moonpool?"

"Goddess of the valley, you are the valley."

"There used to be lake here and that is gone. After that the whole valley was covered with trees, now much of it is fields. I cannot appear if no one believes in me and when they do it is as if they can make me do things."

"Ah, that is what this is about. You went to help Raven and you are guilty because people died."

"And why are holy people always so wise?"

"You are the valley and the valley is peaceful thanks to you, with your help Raven has unified the whole of the peninsular under his leadership. Without you none of this would have been possible. I do not understand your powers but we are nurtured in this valley by you for you are our goddess and we are the people of Moonpool Valley."

"If I am so peaceful how come I helped Raven?"

"You are nature and sometimes nature can appear cruel, but nature is neutral. Creatures do what they need to survive, is that cruel? We also do what we need to survive."

"When Ban came to this valley I stood behind him on this very spot. All was calm then, he was a hunter I know and he needed to kill to live and he wore the skins of animals. But humans kill each other for no reason other than power or greed. I cannot judge, my kind can be as bad. If only I understood the plan but The Maker Of All Things doesn't say. Perhaps you humans have a better idea than I do. After all you are an important part of His plan. But am I important? I am not a part of any plan I am just here. Who am I really?"

"I'm sure Ban would not have settled here without your protection. He knew he was safe here and we are all his heirs and we feel safe here, that must be the plan. You are important and you are Moonpool."

I was not satisfied. I still had the deep yearning so I avoided taking on human form. When Starlight died I felt that deeply. Out of respect for her I took on human form for the ceremony but stood outside the sanctuary. There was still just enough belief in me among the people. I had lost too many friends already and it was becoming more than I could bear so I retreated again. I envied the humans their mortality and wished for some assurance from The Maker Of All Things that my existence counted for something.

I saw the generations come and go, I saw Raven's son Eastwind follow and become Chieftain of the West and Stillwater his sister became chief holy woman of the west. There were other raiders from across the sea but Oengus' heirs remained true to the agreement and Eastwind and his successors continued to defend the land with them. Small homesteads were built up and down the valley and they fared well enough. I continued to watch over them and provide in my natural way but otherwise left them alone. Away from direct human contact this time meant nothing to me and gave me space to reflect without the burden of human emotion. For a space I simply was.

I was aware of a new people in the east who were spreading across the world so I watched and I listened and even in my natural state I found myself waiting.

Chapter 33

Angharad

A stranger stood in the sanctuary. It was about mid-morning. He was tall, taller than any man I had seen, and muscular, his handsome face angular and his expression was oozing with confidence. His hair black as a raven fell about his shoulders. He had a sword of the new metal but it was etched so intricately it was obviously ceremonial rather that made for fighting, this he held point down on the altar, his hands resting of the hilt.

I was strangely drawn to him and stood quietly behind him and waited. He was not waiting, he was just standing, and I was the one who waited. My heart was beating so loudly I was sure he could hear it and this was a totally new experience for me.

"Do I call you Pwll Lleuad or Pwll'euad?" He said without turning, his voice was loud and strong and deep.

This was the new language, not vastly different to the old language but there were significant differences, I had made a point of learning it when I knew the Celts were coming. Moonpool or Pwll Lleuad in their language did sound a little strange I must admit. I didn't answer. There was something magnetic about him, about his voice, I wasn't sure I could trust my voice not to waver.

He turned.

"Oh, no. Certainly not either. Its meaning might very well be romantic but it doesn't sound well. A beautiful goddess like you ought to have a beautiful name. I know, I will call you Angharad."

I felt a thrill through my whole body as he spoke the new name to me. I found that I was dressed in green, a fresh green as the new grass in spring, and my hair was auburn as the leaves of autumn. Not being able to see myself I wondered what else had changed.

"And I am Llewellyn."

His dark eyes pierced through to my innermost being and his smile made me feel weak at the knees. Again I couldn't trust myself to speak because my heart was all aflutter.

"Come." He held out his left hand to me. "Our chariot awaits."

I laid my hand in his and me took me by the hand and lead me out of the sanctuary to a two wheeled cart made for two people to stand in. Two proud horses stood waiting, tossing their manes, ready. We got in, he placed his sword into a loop on the rim of the chariot, with one hand he took up the reins his other stayed on the hilt of his sword. He gave the reins a snap and clicked his tongue and we were off.

"I will tell you what will be now that I and my people are here. I will teach your people the new ways, the better ways and they will be thankful to me for it."

As we passed Village Ban some of the inhabitants stopped what they were doing and watched us pass.

"You have been good to these people but look at them, they live in the past." He said over his shoulder to me. "Don't worry, I will look after them now. I have many things I can give them, new ways of farming, new tools, I can make their lives so much better. This is why I have come personally."

We drove on up the hill, past the point where I had first seen Ban at the shore of the lake.

"We are building a proper road, it will come right across here and it will make trade both east and west so much easier, it will cut travel time and we will become far more prosperous."

We continued on up to a level place overlooking much of the valley. Here were some of his people building round houses on a new site. I wondered that they had just come here without any opposition, I couldn't have been watching that closely. It appeared that he hadn't attacked anyone but had simply settled his people on a new site.

"Welcome to Sarnlas." Which means green causeway. "This is my camp and from here I will oversee all our people. Yours and mine, together they will be one people and we will rule them together."

We dismounted.

"Come, I will show you to my people." He stopped, turned to me and smiled that disarming smile. "Our people."

They were five and five and two men and five and three women. They had already built one of the larger round houses and were in the process of building a second.

"This is Angharad." He announced, thumping his hand heavily on my shoulder so I flinched a little which was a shock especially considering what I was. "Goddess of the valley, we worship at your feet Angharad. Come and see what improvements we make over those simple huts in the valley."

He guided me into the house and stooped a little as he entered behind.

"Sit and be at home, my home is your home."

He led me to one of two chairs in the centre. There were four beds against the walls and a piece of furniture that was new, it had shelves and compartments and all sorts of plates and bowls were displayed on it.

"What is your need? Food, drink, anything you ask I will give you."

I sat. His force of character was overwhelming and I was still afraid to speak.

"No." I managed rather faintly, trembling. "I need nothing."

"Then you will excuse me, I have tasks to perform. I will send Bronwen in to wait on you, anything you want just command her."

He left the house and I let out a long breath I didn't realise I had been holding. I had not had much human contact for some time now and this was quite intense, in fact it was more than intense but I didn't want to admit what it was at that point.

A young woman entered, she was tall and lithe, her hair as black as Llewellyn's, her eyes dark and deep but kindly.

"Welcome Angharad." She bowed low and the whole time she spoke to me she kept her eyes down. "What do you think of my brother?"

"Llwellyn? He's quite a man isn't he." I said, my voice still sounded rather weak.

"Is there anything I can get you? Food, drink?" She paused a moment in thought. "Do you eat and drink?"

"I can, but I never have, not yet anyway."

"Would you like to try something?"

"Not just now thank you Bronwen, I really couldn't."

"If you do then just call. If you will excuse me for a while I have much to do but I will come back soon."

Bowing low again she left me for a while.

For some time I stood in the entrance to the house. I watched Llewellyn stride to and fro, telling his people what to do and when, driving them on to complete the second house. Every once in a while he looked over at me and smiled and every time I thought my heart would stop. He had such a commanding presence I felt there was nothing his people wouldn't do for him. The day wore on and they began to unpack some provisions from a large cart and lay them on mats on the ground. They lit a fire as the Sun began to sink and brought out the two chairs from the house and placed them close to it. Then they began to sit in a large circle on the ground round the fire.

Llewellyn came over to me and held out his hand.

"Come, Angharad, this feast is in honour of you, to welcome you into our midst, you are no longer alone and apart, you are family and you belong."

How had he seen the need that had been growing in me for such a long time? How could he discern my innermost desire?

I put my hand in his and led me towards the two chairs. The people all stood in silence for a moment, bowed to me reverently before sitting again.

"Sit yourself down in place of honour by my side."

He patted my bottom, and this was such a strange sensation for me. I knew what it meant and for a human to think of me in a sexual way was startling but not unwelcome. I sat and he sat on the other chair beside me. I couldn't take my eyes off him the whole evening. Was this possible? Had I found love? Was this the man I would willingly become human for? Was he the answer to all my deep yearnings?

All evening he talked and laughed with everyone and every so often would look at me and smile and hold my hand.

Food and drink was passed around. There were clay jars of fermented grape from far, far away and people drunk freely from them and everyone became merrier as the evening wore on. I touched none of this, perhaps when I became fully human I would feel hunger and thirst but not now. The greatest need I had at that point was being met by the company, by him.

"Eat something Angharad." He would say. "At least have some wine."

But whatever he passed me I would pass on to Bronwen who sat on the ground beside me. She was gazing up at me and I saw awe in her eyes which reminded me of what I was. I didn't want awe and I didn't want to be what I was. I yearned to be with Llewellyn, I so wanted to be human. I wanted to live in the moment and be one with mortal people.

It was very late when the celebration began to slowly come to an end. People began to drift away one at a time. He stood, rather unsteadily.

"We must to bed." He said, his voice very slurred. "I have urgent business in the east and I must start early."

He turned to me. "You must be patient my love, I need to rest tonight and clear my head for I have a long journey ahead of me." He was so unsteady at this moment, almost falling over a couple of times that I doubted he could have done anything anyway.

With that we all went into the two houses where there were beds for everyone including me. Llewellyn flopped onto his and was asleep within moments. However, I do not sleep for as yet I was not human but I watched and I thought and I felt. I allowed myself to feel at last, I opened up my heart and remembered all the people I have been close to and had lost and I allowed myself to mourn. As he lay sleeping I saw the strength in him. He had called me his love and that was enough. I would put Moonpool behind me, now I would be Angharad and I would be his. Was this why Sunlight had foreseen that I would not be remembered, could this be the choice I was to make and if Moonpool makes way for Angharad there would be no Moonpool to remember. Certainly the idea filled me with hope, Moonpool was no longer needed, and I was now free to choose my own destiny.

Chapter 34

Choice

In the morning as the Sun rose he awoke, dressed and went out into the bright day. He blinked and held his head feeling rather the worse for the evening before. I followed. His horse had already been prepared. Just before he got up onto the horse he turned to me, grabbed me about my waist and kissed me full on the lips a long, lingering kiss that took my breath away. But I was too startled to respond.

"This is a promise. Wait for me."

With that he leapt onto his horse in a swift, easy movement. Then he was galloping away down into the mist of the valley.

I stood for ages. The mist in the valley reminded me of the lake but it was not the lake it was only an illusion. It reminded me of how much I had lost over the long years and how I wished never to lose anything again. I could almost feel my physical body becoming more real and my spiritual self slowly slipping away. I remembered Little Rainbow and I prayed to The Maker Of All Things that he would accept me when the time came, but he was silent.

I realised that I had not heard from any of my kind, had I already come this far into full humanity? It was a strange sensation, to not hear the singing of the Sun, the chatter of the smaller spirits of tree and flower and leaf and river. I hoped I had become practically human, if I can become fully human over time rather than suddenly then I won't miss the spiritual so much and hopefully the effect on the valley would be minimal. In any case at that point I no longer cared, the world of people felt so much more real to me, I was no longer looking in from outside, I belonged, at long last I belonged.

The people of the camp had cut down many trees and were using metal spikes and hammers to split them, then long knives to shape them into planks. They took them down into the valley where they were laying a road back towards the east, if the intention was to go all the way to Sea Fort which now was Môrddin under the Celts this was going to take a long time. Perhaps other people were working on the road in each of the villages all the way back, they were an organised people.

Bronwen tentatively came to me, there was still awe in her eyes and she bowed, not daring to look directly at me.

"Your holiness, is there anything I can get for you? You surely must be hungry or thirsty by now."

I did indeed have a strange sensation in my stomach, of course I had a stomach in this form but it had never drawn attention to itself before, but I didn't think it was hunger because the idea of food was a little repulsive at that moment.

"Please don't call me that, call me Angharad as your brother does. I couldn't eat anything at the moment thank you. You can tell me though, what sort of a man is your brother Bronwen?"

"He's a good man, a strong man. He can command people and they obey."

"Do you know what business he has in the east?"

"He has gone to Môrddin where our elder brother intends to be Chieftain over all the west."

"That would include us here then?"

"Yes. Back beyond Môrddin and right out to the far coast and to the North as well. "

"And your brother would then be a sort of under chief to oversee things here. And how far would his territory extend?"

I felt she moved a little uneasily and avoided looking even in my direction. "Yes, Garwain has the utmost confidence in him and would entrust him with the land from here to the coast."

"So, as a person, what sort of a man is Llewellyn?"

"He is a good man. People respect him"

"Yes, but do people like him? Is he kind?"

"If you are worried about him you have no need to, he will be back this evening."

"What sort of a brother is he to you? Is he loving?"

"Can I get you anything at all? Perhaps something to drink, you must be thirsty."

I didn't set any store by her evasiveness because I wasn't asking for any particular reason except I was hoping he was the one, she was his sister and in all probability soon to be my sister too, perhaps she didn't feel it was her place to say too much since she didn't know much about me and was not sure of my intentions. I may be becoming gradually more human but I had been a spirit before the foundations of the earth and that must be somewhat daunting. Besides, I had seen it so often that siblings didn't always get on with each other.

I did wonder if I could help with the road at all, but in human form I have no skills and I am not sure of my physical strength or endurance. As spirit I could have been invaluable but I believed that was slipping away and I didn't want to hang on to any of it. I looked forward to finding out what I could do as a human, I had watched so many tasks being done I was sure I could pick something up. Bronwen oversaw the work that was done and I could see from the way people responded to her that they liked her, she led by example and that is always a good thing.

The day dragged on, for someone who had seen the ice come and go and come and go over the face of the earth, for someone who had seen the first humans after the last time the ice went and had watched them develop and grow over so many generations it did seem strange for one day to feel so long, is this what it is like to be human? Is this what time feels like? But having my insides churned up didn't help. I kept sighing and pacing up and down, I sat in the house and I came out and watched the road builders, I just couldn't be still.

The Sun had set when finally I heard the sound of galloping hooves in the valley. Llewellyn was almost asleep on the horse when he rode into the camp. The horse was covered in sweat and foaming at the mouth, his eyes blazing. I took hold of the horse's reins and was just quick enough to catch Llewellyn as he fell exhausted. I bore his weight easily enough, I was stronger than I thought because he is such a large man and I am only slight. I took him into the house and laid him on his bed.

Bronwen ran in almost in a panic, she was out of breath because she had run all the way up from the road building.

"What is it? Is he alright?" She gasped.

"He is perfectly alright. He is just exhausted." I was still nature spirit enough to know this much, I could feel the life in him.

"Oh, what sort of a day could he have had?"

I stood back and let her tend him. She started removing his heavy coat and his outer clothes. Placing his items of jewellery on the wooden shelves by his bed and folding his clothes in a pile on the floor. She pulled a blanket over him. She went out and fetched his sword from the horse and laid it by his side on the bed.

"Are you sure he is alright?" She asked again much calmer having tended to him.

"I know these things, I feel the life in him, he is simply exhausted. All he needs now is to sleep and he will be well and rested in the morning."

Only then did I remember the horse, there had been no one around to tend him. I went outside and I lay my hand on his flank and calmed him down, then I led him round to the enclosure behind the house where I brushed him down carefully and thoroughly with dry straw and pulled a coarse blanket over him. Then I placed some grain on a mat for him which he ate. Soon he lay down quietly and rested. But he was afraid of something and I couldn't piece together his thoughts.

Soon afterwards everyone came up from the road where they had been eating. They paid little attention to Llewellyn's return and simply settled in for the night. I went back into the house but I was still unable to sleep for as yet I had no need. So I watched Llewellyn sleep. It is said that a person reveals their true face while they sleep.

I noticed a strange twist to Llewellyn's mouth which I had not seen the previous night. Perhaps things had gone well that day for him and it was a smile of satisfaction and I was glad. I eagerly awaited the morning to hear his news and more importantly to at last begin our life together, even planning the ceremony. But a day of unsettled waiting made the night dreadfully long and in the state I was in I couldn't simply wait. And all the time the horses thought played at the back of my mind.

So after a long time as the night drew on I absently began to finger his trinkets on the shelves, especially the items he had been wearing. Among them there was a bronze clasp and a leather cord that went round his neck. On the cord was a bronze hoop intertwined with what seemed like human hair.

"Whose hair is this?" I pondered out loud.

I don't know what had happened in Môrddun or the importance of the hair but Llewellyn must have been ready to spring into action as a result because the moment I spoke he jumped up, sword in hand. He swung it at me and could have perhaps killed me only I jumped back just as quickly, he still caught my arm. It wasn't a deep cut fortunately but just enough to draw blood, and the intense burning dropped me to my knees. I was in agony and it wasn't that I hadn't felt pain before and therefore this was a new experience, this was much more than that, a burning pain that shot through my whole body, my right arm was numb and lifeless with it.

"Oh, Angharad!" Llewellyn exclaimed. "I am so sorry, you startled me, did I hurt you?"

With effort I stood, how I didn't faint with the pain I don't know. I still held the cord in my left hand and I lifted it in front of me, I felt this was significant.

"Whose hair is this?" I asked as calmly as I could, trying not to grit my teeth.

He looked blankly at me for a moment, not because he didn't know but he didn't know how to answer.

"Forget that." He said. "Are you alright? I was dreaming, I didn't know it was you."

There was guilt in his eyes. I didn't know what had happened but I was sure it had something to do with why he sprang at me and I then began to be even more suspicious of the hair.

"Whose hair is this?" I demanded.

"Give me that." He went to grab it, anger on his face and his eyes blazed.

In that instance realisation flooded over me, he was not who I thought he was. Suddenly I saw a scheming man, a violent man. Before he managed to grab the cord from my hand my hair became dark almost as the night itself, my skin pale as the Moon, my eyes blue and deep as the still waters, my raiment silver at my shoulders fading to a deep, deep blue below my knees. He stopped short seeing he had lost his hold over me.

"Angharad, my love, what is this? Do you not trust me?" But the fire had not gone out of his eyes.

He was used to human women and although I yearned to be human I was not, I am a nature spirit and I am older than the earth itself. In my anger I grew to twice my size. The pain in my arm was so intense it seemed only the fire of my anger being stronger than the fire in my arm kept me going.

"Whose hair is this?" I demanded loudly.

"My wife's." He said lowering his eyes, unable to hide anything from me. "But she is dead."

"And is her blood also on your sword?"

"Angharad, all I have done is for you, I am yours. I have cleared the way that we may rule the whole of Demetae, you and I, we will be the greatest rulers and our children and their children after them."

"I am not Angharad I am Moonpool or Pwll'euad if you prefer and I do not wish to rule."

My wings, dark as the night loomed over him and he cowered beneath me. And finally seeing him as he was, small and human and fragile and a liar and a murderer my anger abated, I could hold the physical form no longer because of the intense burning through my whole being and I was gone.

Chapter 35

Reflection

"Where am I?"

I gazed before me but could make nothing out. The land before me was silvery grey strewn with rock and dust. The Sun was far too bright, brighter than I thought possible and there were stars in the black, black sky that shouldn't be while the Sun was out. My arm was still on fire and I wasn't sure if I was in spirit or physical form.

"You are safe." Silverwheel said beside me.

A blue green dome hung in the sky, mottled with white, I gazed at this as I knew I should recognise it but for a moment I couldn't place it. Then I realised what it was, it was the part of the earth illuminated by the Sun. It was a long time since I had seen it from outside, from the depths of space. And as for the land about me, I was on the surface of the Moon.

"Yes, we are on the Moon my dear Moonpool."

Pain, anguish, hurt, and a myriad other emotions flooded over me and I sank to the ground and sobbed bitterly. Silverwheel stooped down with me, she put her arms around me and let me cry. Eventually she spoke.

"The burning pain in your arm is because the sword was iron and I am afraid this new metal has that effect on us, avoid it at all costs. You will feel it in all forms you take but it will fade with time. The hurt to your heart goes deeper than that, not for the useless braggart but for the deep yearning you had and now you realise is futile, you will never be human, we only have one choice and you came close."

"Silverwheel. Why didn't you warn me? Why didn't you stop me?"

"You closed yourself to us all, you remember Little Rainbow? It was your choice, your one choice and we could not interfere."

She let me cry.

After a while she tried to lighten the mood and cheer me up a little.

"Do you realise that with these new people I am Arianrhod. But then I have so many names all over the world."

I managed a little chuckle. "It's better than Pwll'euad, it is the only one I have."

"Yes, you will have to put up with that too. But you know the passing of time, a new people and a new language will follow, your eventual name will be the prettiest of the lot."

"You can see the future?"

"I am allowed to know some things. Sunlight told you that your name would be forgotten which must trouble you and didn't help just now, but you have made your choice and you do have a future and you name will be remembered in time, the name you will have then."

She smoothed my hair and wiped my tears. I looked at my arm. The cut was gone because my human form is not really human at all and the form we were in was somewhere in between yet even in this form the angry redness remained. I looked up at the Sun.

"Is Lleu Llaw Gyffes happy with his name?"

"He has so many names too. But in this case, to borrow a phrase from the humans he is over the Moon."

We both laughed.

"But why could I have been so stupid? How could I be taken in so easily?"

"Our role is a lonely one, we are not human and we are not messengers, we are guardians. My home is here but I have freedom to roam yet still I am lonely. You are the valley and have to contend with whoever comes to you and you rarely see beyond. Of course you see what the human have even though you know it is so fragile and short and ever since you met Ban you have wanted to be one with them, it is such a deep yearning with many of us but it was very strong with you because you are a kind spirit and have been close to the people. It is less with me because I cannot be close to them, yet I still have it. I was afraid we had lost you to it and there was really nothing I could do."

"So in a way I was lucky Llewellyn struck me with the sword."

"Actually he struck you three times. There is a magic within us that a man only need to strike us three times and even if we become fully human we still revert to our spirit selves."

"Three times? Once only, surely,"

"Once on your shoulder, once on your bottom and you know the third."

"But the first two were hardly strikes."

"Spirits have left for less."

"So how did Little Rainbow not return? Did Uban never strike her, or pat her?"

"Not roughly and not with greed in his heart, he was the most tender of men and he truly loved her deeply and not for what he would gain from her."

"And Llewellyn do you mean he was hoping to gain something from me all along? Are you saying he never loved me?"

"If it helps then no, he never loved you. He had heard of a nature spirit in your valley where many others have been forgotten and knew that if he could entice you to mate with him he would be chieftain of the whole area. Such is the power we have without knowing it. He believed you were as good as his, he believed he had won you over, so he went to Sea Fort or Môrddin as it is now and killed his brother and the only other person who stood in his way."

"His wife."

"He should have taken you last night but he was too exhausted, he would have this morning. Look!" She pointed at the Earth. "Your valley is coming into the sunlight now. Soon the men from his brother's court who have been riding through the night will be on him and as he has not mated with a spirit he has no power over them, they will take him back and execute him, and you do not want to see that. You do know they will execute him three times. Humans can be so cruel."

"I have seen the cruel things humans can do. But I should be there."

"No you should not! Not yet anyway. You most certainly should not be there for him and it would not be in your nature to see him executed. You have seen war but this you do not want to see."

"Should I go back to my valley then?"

"Watch the Earth roll on for a while longer, when your valley rolls into the afternoon then you can appear in the sanctuary and summon the four camps to you. Pronounce Bronwen as their leader, they all need the new Celtic learning, moreover since the Celts have come they need to live together, better to have someone you trust and will listen to you. Otherwise more will come and there may be bloodshed. Rename Stillwater of Ban's village Gwybod and send him to the newly updated Oak Thicket now called Clunderwen in their tongue to train as a druid, which is much as the holy people were before but with much greater learning. Hopefully we can keep the peace and give them a purpose into the future as the old races and the new mingle and all become Celtic. After all, they are not that dissimilar and there are many family connections already."

We stood, then. I would have taken a deep breath but there is no air on the Moon.

Suddenly she took my face in her hands and it was her turn to cry.

"Oh Moonpool! Moonpool, my daughter I was so afraid I had lost you. I saw the light go out of your eyes and it cut me to the depths of my being."

She looked intently into my eyes and I managed a weak smile.

"But, there, there you are Moonpool once more."

"But who is Moonpool, I am different each time someone has faith for me to appear, who is Moonpool if I reflect the wishes of the people all the time?"

"You are the valley and the valley is rock and soil and water and growing things. But as the humans live there and tend the land you and the valley grow and change with them but remain the valley and Moonpool. We and nature are one and whatever advances humanity makes we adapt with them, but we are stronger and for all their advances they cannot change us. You have power you do not understand but you are a gentle and kind spirit and you will never abuse it."

"Do you think they will ever come here?"

"Here? The Moon you mean? What for, there is nothing they want here."

"They are proud and arrogant. They might come just to say they did."

"I can't see how it is possible."

Chapter 36

Pwll'euad

I was in the sanctuary, the Sun was bright and the air was still. I stood still and listened, listened to the river gurgling in its bed, listened to the birds singing in the trees, listened to the small animals scurrying and sniffing, listened to the very growing of the grass. I breathed deeply and smelled the earth, it was rich and moist and abundantly fruitful. This is who I am. And as if I needed to be reminded of this my arm still burned because of the contact with iron, something humans don't suffer from.

I am not very tall for an earth spirit and this hadn't been a problem before because I wasn't far short of Ban and taller than many of his descendants. But many of the newcomers were quite a bit taller than me and I needed to make an impression. I could double my size but I wasn't angry enough. I knew Bronwen was in awe of me so I could use her belief to try something out before they came.

I wondered whether my wings were substantial enough to bear my weight as they are not like the feathered wings of the messengers. So I unfurled my dark butterfly wings as wide as I could, I began to flap them which I had never tried before. It was quite a wonderful feeling but nothing happened, they were not strong enough to lift me. Then I adjusted my own weight and soon began to hover in the air a few feet off the ground. This would be enough since I wouldn't need to fly about. Then I settled back onto the ground rather pleased with myself and having enjoyed the experience.

With my feet firmly planted on the ground I pressed my toes into the soil and reached out as the valley to all who dwelt within it, summoning them to my presence. This was not a compulsion but a request, but because it was in the very soil of the valley the humans wouldn't realise why they felt the need to be here so would hopefully come without question.

And they did. I hadn't realised just how many people lived in the valley now, they filled the sanctuary and overflowed beyond. So it was just as well I could hover above them while the Sun past the height of noon and slowly sinking to the west glinted on my wings.

"People of the valley. I am Moonpool though in the new language I am Pwll'euad and I am the spirit of the valley where you live. I have appeared to you because this is a moment of choice and an opportunity for peace. You may be different peoples but you are all people of the valley because you have all chosen to be here and settle here and you need to be one people, you all need each other as we go into the future. Those of you who have come here from away need the people already here. You need their understanding of the land and their hard work and skills. Those of you who have always been here need the people who have come here. You need their experience, their knowledge and their new tools and new skills."

They just all stood, open mouthed, men, women and children, gazing up at me.

"Bronwen, come to the altar."

There was a disturbance some distance back, her people were holding her back, they must have thought I wanted to punish her, after what her brother had done and after all it was only this morning he had been taken away.

"Let her through." Some of my people insisted, also assuming there would be some punishment.

In the end she pushed through her own people and the others parted to let her pass. She came trembling to the altar and knelt, expecting the worse but ready to face whatever was to come. I floated to the ground, stood beside her and placed my hands on her head.

"Bronwen. You are chief of Pwll'euad Valley, it is up to you what other communities you can win to yourself, but your role here is to govern and direct all the people of this valley."

I floated up again on my wings and gazed over the people.

"If anyone has any objections I will listen fairly."

"She has no right, hers are a new people and we are the children of Ban." Braveheart of Ban said calmly in the old tongue though I knew he could speak Celtic.

"No, she has no right." I answered in Celtic. "I do not say she has the right, what I say is this, the Celts will come in greater number and will not care for you as she will, she is the leader you need. I offer you this advice which you do not have to take. I have made her chief, accept her because she is the best leader and she will bring all peoples together and lead you into the future.

Reject her and someone else will come to subjugate you, I cannot hold all these people back if they come. And neither could Arianrhod."

Braveheart bowed his head. "I accept your wisdom Moonpool." Then he continued in the Celtic tongue. "Pwll'euad is right, Bronwen is our chief."

There was no loud cheering only silence. Then the Celts started a chant of "Bronwen, Bronwen." But the others didn't join in.

"Stillwater." I called out as I sank back to the ground and folded away my wings.

Braveheart brought the young son of Crow of Vellon Village, Stillwater, to me at the altar.

"Stillwater. You are a special boy, you should go to Clunderwen and train to be a Druid, the blood of Little Rainbow is in you as is the blood of Ban, you have shown wisdom beyond your years so take on the Celtic name of Gwybod and you shall be the wise man you are meant to be."

Braveheart looked at me properly for the first time. He saw the wisdom of this for though the chief was the leader of a people the advice of a druid was where the real power lay and there would be balance between the old people and the new.

"His training will take many years, Braveheart, you must aid and advise Bronwen in the meantime, she doesn't know your people or your history and if she is to lead all the people she will need your help."

This I said to Braveheart alone, many of the people had taken up the chant, "Stillwater, Stillwater." Then they added somewhat reluctantly, "Bronwen." As well.

Chapter 37

Collaboration

Braveheart came to the sanctuary in the night and he stood, looking up at the stars. He was clearly waiting so I felt myself drawn in to mortal affairs again though for the present as spirit. And this time I had no yearning to be human. He whistled quietly to himself a tune that the people building the road had been singing a few days before while they worked and I wondered at this. A short time later Bronwen also came and they stood side by side in front of the altar to watch the Sun rise. The winter was just beginning and the weather had been mixed of late but today promised to be a bright day.

They were clearly drawn to each other but as yet neither of them was aware. At this point it was simply a matter of two people trying to forge two communities into one and they both needed the others advice and insight.

"Tell me of Moonpool." Said Bronwen as the sky grew lighter in the east and the stars began to fade.

"I really can't tell you much, I never actually saw her before. Of course we have always revered her, she knew Ban and has featured in our stories through the ages but until I actually saw her I wasn't entirely sure if stories were all that she was. Now I see that there is an actual goddess behind the stories."

"Secretive is she?"

"Perhaps, it must be so."

"Mysterious?"

"In your experience how does she compare to other gods and goddesses?"

"She is the first I have actually met."

"But you have much experience of the world, you come from beyond the sea, you must know something, heard stories."

"Yes, indeed, like you, I have heard stories and thought that is all they were. My brother was the one who believed the stories and I often teased him about it. He knew that if he were to marry a goddess he would have great wealth and power because there are stories where that has happened. Until now I never believed them."

"Now, we must both rethink what we know. Who knows what Moonpool is capable of."

"I don't know what she did to my brother. But I must admit I am afraid of her."

"Your brother believed you say."

Braveheart looked at her trying to gauge her reaction to his death. She saw him turn and turned to him. Their eyes met for a moment then she looked back at the bright first appearance of the Sun on the horizon.

"My brother was an evil man. I do not mourn his death if that is what you are wondering."

"Even so, he was still your brother."

"I had two brothers. My other brother was such a good man, the eldest son, Llewellyn was always jealous." At this she was sad and a tear came to her eye. "I miss him and hate Llewellyn for murdering him."

"I am so sorry." He gave her upper arm a slight squeeze.

She sighed and drew in a breath.

"Moonpool can be fierce can't she, quite apart from what she did to Llewellyn."

"There are tales of her fighting our enemies. Then this must be true as well."

"Oh." The colour drained from her face for a moment, but only a moment. "But then since she appointed me chief, she doesn't see us as enemies, I hope it means she has accepted us into her valley."

"Yes, she wants us to work together. If people come in peace they have always been made welcome, this is necessary for our growth." His hand was still on her arm.

She looked at him again, he was gazing at her, their eyes met, and she looked back as the Sun rose into the sky.

"When she was Angharad she looked different, not so much in her face. She seemed different somehow. I can't quite work out how. What was that about? And when she went for LLewellyn…! He was a quivering wreck after that and my cousin's men had no trouble leading him off. I know what he was after but I don't understand her, was it some kind of test on her part? Was she playing with him, with us?"

"Gods are mysterious. If it was a test then he didn't pass and you did."

"I suppose. Then we must work together, I wouldn't want to be on the wrong side of her."

"I know the land and I know the people, you know the world and the new tools. I'll see if I can get you some help with the road, you're not building it all the way to Môrddin are you?"

"Just as far as the next settlement, the people there will continue on. I wonder what has happened in Môrddin." She became very withdrawn. "I wonder if I should have gone."

"We will hear news soon enough, do you have other close relatives or are you head of your family now?"

"I have a cousin, Arwel, if they have any sense they will make him Chieftain. It is not something I would aspire to."

"It is probably time we sent some more building materials there, our traders can find out while they are there. Have you got someone you can send with them who will know what sort of tools we need and can do some asking around?"

They were both quiet again for some time, watching the sun rise in the sky, listening to the camps coming alive and the sound of hammers working on the road.

"Is there anything useful to the south, beyond Pole's Camp?" Asked Bronwen.

"We haven't had much to do with the people there."

"Then it is time we did, this would seem to me an important central place. We ought to build a bridge across the river here rather than wading across all the time."

"It would need to be a strong bridge for the river tends to flood at times. We have tried before but anything that has been built in the past has got washed away."

"With nails of iron we could build one strong enough."

Braveheart was still holding her arm. "We do make a good team."

She looked at him and smiled and they held each other's gaze for a significant time.

Chapter 38

Acceptance

Doithineb, the druid from Môrddin, stood in the sanctuary facing the altar. Only a faint glow in the east announced the approach of the morning Sun. He stood silently, feeling the space, reaching out to me with his mind but not enough to actually summon me. Everyone was a little scared of me. This was the spring equinox with which the sanctuary was aligned. He knew this was a very important day for everyone. It was a day that marked the beginning of the future. The two peoples would become one and they would all be Celts at last.

The road was almost complete from Môrddin to here and it was planned to take it further into the west. New ploughs had been brought in made of iron and wood and more areas of the land were being sown with barley. The bridge had been built and had survived the winter floods needing only a few minor repairs. The communities had weathered the winter together and many friendships had been made. A new trade link had been made to the south. But today was an important day.

As the sky grew lighter Doithineb heard the people approach, there was singing and dancing and laughter and beating of drums and blowing of horns and reeds. Then silence fell as they reached the entrance of the sanctuary.

As the first rays of the Sun broke over the hill he turned. He turned and held his arms wide in greeting.

"Bronwen, Braveheart, enter."

Bronwen was robed in a long flowing gown of green from her shoulders to the ground, a hood over her head. Braveheart had on his bronze armour polished so it gleamed in the rising sunlight. They entered the sanctuary and approached Doithineb. Bronwen's cousin, Arwel Chieftain of Môrddin and the west, was wearing armour of leather and iron and he followed after with the rest of the people following him.

Doithineb addressed the people in a loud voice. "Brothers and sisters, Bronwen and Braveheart have come to this holy place to pledge their lives to each other before the gods and all the people. In their union is also the union of the two peoples. This is a joyous occasion because it is the culmination of their flowering love for each other and the promise of life for the future."

He turned and took a golden torque from the altar and handed it to Braveheart who then placed in round Bronwen's neck.

"I Braveheart give this symbol of my love to you Bronwen as I give my life to you."

Doithineb then took a cloak from the altar and handed it to Bronwen who then placed it over Braveheart's shoulders and fastened it with a golden clasp.

"I Bronwen give this symbol of my love to you Braveheart as I give my life to you."

Doithineb then directed them to place their right hands together. He tied their wrists with a cord of woven wool dyed with many colours.

"Braveheart, will you take Bronwen as your own, to love and protect her and to share your life and all you have with her?"

"I so promise."

"Bronwen, will you take Braveheart as your own, to love and protect him and to share your life and all you have with him?"

"I so promise."

He directed them to kneel.

"Therefore I declare before the gods and this people that they are husband and wife, their lives are one from this day forward. Bronwen and Braveheart receive the blessing of the gods and your ancestors and all the people gathered, and receive my blessing too. May the blessing give you children that they may continue from your love into a bright future."

They stood and kissed amid loud clapping and cheering.

Arwel stepped forward, turned to the people and raised his hands and waited for silence.

"I, Arwel, Chieftain of Demetae, declare that in this union we are one people. I will treat you all equally. My daughter, Bronwen, will judge and lead the people of this valley with my full authority and with the aid of the wisest of all men, Braveheart who has already proved a worthy man in so many ways. This day I have provided a banquet so rejoice, eat, drink and celebrate."

And so, with loud shouts and cheers the couple were borne aloft and all the people went to the flat plain to the east of the sanctuary where tents had been set up, food and drink in profusion had been laid on and there was music and dancing and singing.

I had been invited, Bronwen particularly had asked me when she came to the sanctuary the day before but I had simply whispered without appearing that this was a day for people and not spirits, that this was their future. I was glad for them and glad for myself. There would be peace for the moment apart from the constant raids from Irene the land beyond the sea. With Môrddin as the capital of Demetae all the land and all the peoples were one people, the marriage between Bronwen and Braveheart did much to make this happen not just within the valley but throughout the territory.

One thing I did think it wise to suggest to Bronwen, so I spoke to her some days later when she stood alone in the sanctuary.

"Bronwen, I know there is peace and stability, yet I fear for the future. I think it would be wise to build fortresses, one far up in the narrow valley of the Gronw and one on the hills overlooking the Marlais on the border between me and Arberth."

Bronwen looked at me sadly. "This I have already been thinking of too, Moonpool."

"Then why do you look so sad?"

"You didn't come. I was afraid I would not see you again."

"You are one of the last. My time is coming to an end, you do not need me."

"But ..."

"No, you mortals are quite capable of seeing to your own destiny."

"I don't want to say goodbye to you, surely this is not our last meeting. Will I see you again?"

"There is no need but we may yet talk."

"I am glad I got to know you properly."

I had finally found peace within myself. No longer did I have that deep yearning for I knew that my role was to oversee them and not to be one of them. Having come so close to relinquishing my very nature I now knew this is who I am and who I want to be. To see the people who I care for grow old and die will always be part of the sadness within me but there are always new people to care for and watch over.

Chapter 39

Gwybod

Gwybod stood in the sanctuary in front of the altar facing the east, it was still night and the sky was overcast and starless, it would be some time yet before the Sun rose. The seasons had come and gone many times and now he was fully trained. He wore a simple linen robe belted with a rope of flax under a heavy woollen cloak. He carried the oak staff but had not been awarded the oak crown.

Should I stand with him?

He had come quietly and had carefully avoided any of the villages. He was quite an open person and he was convinced of my existence. I could have appeared to him, I could also have read some of his thoughts but I did neither. Although he was an open person in his soul he wanted to project an air of distance, perhaps even mystery, this much was obvious without reading his thoughts. And he was proud and this was probably why he hadn't been awarded the crown.

A wind blew up, not a strong wind, but there must have been a cold edge to it as he shivered slightly. Some of the autumn leaves were blown from the trees and they floated round and round before settling. The clouds began to break up and clear from the west, the stars began to appear and the Moon past her full.

And still he stood.

The sky began to lighten in the east and when the first rays of the Sun broke over the horizon the cloud had almost cleared so Gwybod was greeted by the Sun in his full glory.

"A sign." He said to himself. "I am accepted."

Accepted by whom? Not by me for he hadn't asked, nor had he asked Lleu or The Maker Of All Things. Should I appear to him now?

But he turned and strode out of the sanctuary and up to Ban's Village, now Pentreban, stood in the middle of the houses and shouted with a voice that seemed a little thin for one of his stature.

"Greetings to you. I am Gwybod and I am returned."

Before anyone had a chance to respond he was off again, up the hill to Sarnlas leaving the people gazing at his retreating figure. There in between the three huts he stood and shouted.

"Greetings. I am Gwybod and I am returned. Bronwen and Braveheart I am here."

A young man emerged from the main house. He stood in front of Gwybod and shouted back with his rich and commanding voice.

"And I am Bleddyn son of Bronwen and Braveheart." Then he laughed. "Gwybod, we have been waiting for you, welcome back, my parents are in Môrddin so you will have to put up with me." He grabbed his right forearm and shook it vigorously.

Gwybod was rather taken aback. "Then what I have to say will have to wait. Build me a hermitage across the valley, up there." He pointed roughly in the direction to the right of Pole's camp, or Pôl Mawr as it had become. "Send them to me there when they return."

"I will get some people on it right away. In the meantime, come in and have something to eat and get warm by the fire."

Without replying Gwybod turned and strode off in the direction he had indicated.

As directed by Gwybod a small stone house was built towards the top of the hill that marked my southern border where there was a good supply of water and he had a good view of much of the valley. And although he hadn't asked Bleddyn arranged for food to be brought to him.

He settled in and the earth turned beneath the Sun two more times before Bronwen and Braveheart returned. Though their primary business had been official to do with the governing of the regions they had taken the cart and had managed to bring more iron tools for digging soil and more grain for sowing. Bleddyn told them that Gwybod had returned and had asked to see them and straight away they went up to see him.

He heard them coming and stood outside his stone hut to meet them. "Braveheart, it is good to see you after such a long time."

"Stillwater, how you have grown, you were only a boy last time I saw you, how long has it been?"

"Twenty years and my name is Gwybod."

"Have you seen your father since you have been back?"

"He came here yesterday."

There was a short silence, Gwybod obviously wasn't going to elaborate.

"Why are you up here alone?" Asked Bronwen. "You should be among the people. We should celebrate your return as a druid."

"I have learned so much." Said Gwybod directing his answer to Braveheart. "I know how to read the signs and see the future, I can advise you. You need my guidance there is much change coming."

"Well, yes, that is part of your role." Said Bronwen. "Things seem settled at the moment. We have just come back from my cousin Arwel and the regional chiefs. Our only threat is from Irene but we are prepared."

"You are not prepared for what is to come, maybe it will not come yet, maybe not for a long time, but there is a power coming that will take over the world and all the old ways will be swept aside."

Bronwen and Braveheart exchanged glances.

"Go, leave me." He said. "Come to me when you are ready to listen."

"We are listening now, tell us." Said Bronwen.

But he spoke no more. He turned his back and gazed towards the east as if he could see the threat approaching in the far distance.

Bronwen and Braveheart stopped in the sanctuary before returning to their camp.

"Do you believe him?" Braveheart asked.

"Yes, there are many peoples in the world, many leaders who wish to dominate. But for the moment they fight each other and we are remote and unimportant."

"Will they come here?"

"Eventually I don't doubt."

"How do we prepare?"

"As we always have, we trade for better tools and weapons, we train our people. We grow and become stronger. We listen to news from afar and keep alert."

"And Moonpool, she has always helped in the past."

"I don't know, Moonpool says this is a time for us and her time is passing."

"Do you think it worth asking her?"

"I will ask."

Chapter 40

Uncertainty

The next day Bronwen came on her own to the sanctuary. She placed more dry wood and grasses in the clay bowl that was always on the altar and lit it from a flint. When she had a good fire going she put some belladonna leaves in. Then she knelt silently at the altar. The Sun was sinking in the west now and the clouds were beginning to gather.

I stood behind her silently, not because she wished it but because I did.

"Moonpool." She used my old name.

"Bronwen. Please stand."

She would not stand, she would not look up.

"Moonpool, is Gwybod right."

"I cannot and will not talk to the top of your head, please stand."

She would not. I did wonder since she was taller than me if she was afraid to stand for she would be looking down at me.

"I am not angry with you, you have nothing to fear." I said in case she was afraid.

She remained kneeling, head bowed. "Moonpool, there are many powers in the world. Is there one in particular we need to fear?"

I knelt down beside her. "You were once a new people to this land and you were a power the people here could have been afraid of. This is a resilient land filled with resilient people as you have seen. Powerful people come and go it is the ordinary people, the people of the land, who make the world. That is the way it has always been and always will be."

"But the future, it is all so uncertain."

"The future is always uncertain for even I do not know the future. I have lived through so many uncertain futures and the people are still here. The blood of Ban has been mixed with so many other peoples but it still runs through the veins of the people here as it does in Bleddyn. You have come as an outsider from a country far away, you have a new language and new ways and yet all the people here are still one people, the people of the valley. You even used my old name."

She looked at me at last. I smiled and she smiled back. She was still taller than me even when we both knelt.

"Gwybod has unsettled you has he not?" I said as I held her gaze.

She didn't answer for a while but was deep in thought.

"There was something about him I couldn't work out, but I didn't like him."

"He hates your people despite learning so much of your knowledge and despite much of what his training is about. Or at the very least he resents your people therefore you must learn to live with that. You are chief here and you must be strong because he will try to force his way on you. You personally must resist him. I don't know why Arianrhod chose him but she did, we must both accept that."

"So how do you find him then?"

It was my turn to look down. I thought for a long time before I answered. I turned back to her and could see she was struggling with some sort of dilemma too.

"He doesn't speak to me." I said. "He is an open person and I could read his thoughts if I wanted to but I won't do that. He is proud but anyone can see that, I'm sure you have. He is too proud even for a druid."

The puzzled look on her face grew.

"I will not interfere." I said. "I am the spirit of the valley, guardian maybe, but I try not to interfere with the natural development of the people here." I chuckled a little at that knowing how much I have interfered over the generations. "Well, I try not to interfere too much."

"You are a goddess but when I talk to you I feel you are my friend. I have to keep reminding myself of who you are."

I sighed and squatted back onto my heels. "I am a creature as you are, I am the valley, the soil beneath your feet, the leaves upon the trees, the river and the stones over which it flows, I am older than the world and I will be here long after you have died but I am still a creature. When I take on this form I feel as you do, in fact my arm is still burning because of your brother, I have a heart that came close to being broken. So of course I am your friend. That is my greatest joy and my greatest sadness, I have had many friends and I have lost many friends, let us be friends for now and I am content."

This startled her for a moment. She also squatted back onto her heels and looked into my eyes. She was still taller than me.

"There is so much about you I do not know. However we go into an uncertain future together?" She said, but this was a rhetorical question. “Then we discover the future as it comes together as friends.”

Tentatively she reached out and took my right hand in both of hers.

“One question…” She began.

“No questions.” I knew the question, it was about her brother.

We knelt together as the Sun went behind a bank of cloud in the west. A cold wind blew down from the north and crows circled in the sky. She shivered slightly.

Chapter 41

Omen

Gwybod stood at the altar, his cloak gathered tight around him. He looked up into the night sky and sang the song of the Sun, pleading that he would be born again after this the longest of nights. The people waited anxiously behind, even though they had been through this year after year there was always the slight worry that the dark gods would overpower the Sun this time especially as they had all heard Gwybod's dire warnings by now. But even so, even now no one was really dull enough to doubt the return of the Sun.

For the third time Gwybod tried to light the fire on the altar but this time I relented and didn't cause the breeze at the wrong time. I am afraid this was a little trick I learned from Arberth. Man on the Bush would have preferred Dynar but this was the name his people called him and the small town that was growing there and he could live with this name and teased me that I was now Pwll'euad and nothing else, not even one of the villages or the river, was called that. We were good friends now even though I could still feel the darkness of unquiet souls fading though they were as a result of the conflict now so distant in the past as almost to have been forgotten.

The flame sputtered but didn't go out.

The sky in the west began to lighten and the stars began to fade. Traces of cloud scuttled across the sky, the broken ends of a larger mass that threatened beyond the horizon.

Gwybod began another chant and the people joined in, a chant of awakening, bidding the Sun to rise and put on his strength again.

Bronwen drew near with a bowl of water and a pouch of coins and as she placed them on the altar the flame flared up in strength and died down again as she withdrew. It guttered and almost went out but just about stayed alight. This was not missed by the people but I was not sure about Gwybod as he was looking up into the sky away from the flame. But this was not my doing, it was the belief of Bronwen and humans are not always aware they have this power.

His eyes were closed in apparent ecstasy as the chanting became more intense. The sky in the east began to cloud over just as the Sun's rays would have broken over the horizon so the spectacle was somewhat muted. Then Gwybod and the people completed their chant but there was no loud roar of voices for although the Sun had risen he was obscured by the cloud. Again the people feared this was an omen.

However, the festivities began as they always had every year. There was singing and dancing, eating and drinking, but the sudden downpour of rain did rather subdue even this, it also put out the flame.

The people began to disperse, Gwybod shouted out that this was an omen then went back to his hermitage. Only Bronwen remained, drawing her cloak over her head. The rain was heavy, more like sleet. It could even turn to snow.

"Moonpool." She said. "I understand why you played tricks with the flame, but did you have to obscure the Sun with the cloud and make it rain?"

"Not all the effects with the flame were my doing, Bronwen, and I did not bring the cloud." I said, standing with her in the sleet. "The spirits of the weather are an unruly bunch and I don't understand their reasoning. You realise this would not have affected us only. Perhaps it is an omen, I have no knowledge of the future but perhaps there will be a new power in the east."

"An omen. Do you know of any power in the east?"

"There are a few as you already know. Any one of them could gain in power but at present they struggle against each other. And as I told you before, it is not the people of power or even the fighters that conquer. They just change the rules. It is ordinary people who are the backbone of humanity. It is them who get on with working and farming and making. The rulers cannot manage without them."

Chapter 42

Passing

Gwybod stood facing the altar. The sky was blue and the summer Sun blazed down on the assembly. A gentle breeze blew up the valley and the fires on the altar blazed brightly.

Bronwen's body lay on the pyre that had been built on top of the bank where Ban lay. The earth had circled the Sun many times and Gwybod and Bronwen had been at odds the whole time, only latterly had relations between them improved. He could see the advantages that the Celts had brought and realised that if the two peoples had not joined his people would have been pushed to one side and be left behind.

In all this time he had not acknowledged me or any of the spirits, not even The Maker Of All Things. He had kept to himself mostly up in his little hermitage. Maintaining the ceremonies, healing the sick, offering advice but mostly to Braveheart and usually from up on the hill. The threat from the east still had not come and there was still relative peace, he continued to warn of this but people no longer took him seriously.

He took a torch and lit it in the left hand flame. He took the torch round to the pyre.

"Bronwen. You have proved yourself a wise and capable leader. You have earned the respect of all the peoples of the valley and have earned the right to rest with Ban."

This was indeed a huge thing for him to admit. He thrust the torch into the pyre, slowly at first the wood began to burn, and then suddenly it blazed fiercely causing him to step back.

He came back round the altar.

"Bleddyn, come forth."

Bleddyn stepped from the people and knelt before Gwybod.

"Bleddyn." Gwybod took a flask from his belt, removed the stopper and poured oil on Bleddyn's head. "Your mother has passed and now I anoint you Chief of our people under the authority of Gareth, son of Arwel, Chieftain of Môrddin and Demetae. Rise and rule your people in justice and in love."

He stood and Gwybod took the sword from the altar and placed it in his hand and then took the cloak and put it over his shoulders fastening it with the gold broach. Bleddyn turned and held the sword aloft.

"Bleddyn, Bleddyn." The people chanted.

I physically stood at the back, unnoticed by all, and wept. Unseen by all except Braveheart, and it was because of his belief in me that I was there. He was old and frail and only able to attend at all because I had brought him though not by walking. And before anyone saw us we were back in his house and I lay him back down.

"I am sorry Moonpool." He said weakly, his breath short and shallow. "Gwybod won't acknowledge you and Bleddyn listens to him."

"I have been through all that before. I have been forgotten for many generations but I am the valley and I remain. Maybe I have interfered too much and not always let your people develop as they should. Your people have grown so much since I first met Ban and I am not sure that I need to be seen."

He held my hand. "If you had not interfered there would have been bloodshed and I wonder if our people would have survived. You have been more than the valley, you have been a friend."

I did wonder if his would be the last human hand I would ever hold. Humanity was changing, growing away from us. I hoped they hadn't finished with us yet though I knew many of my kind had all but fallen asleep. I had talked to Bronwen about losing so many friends but this time so much more was passing.

"Goodbye Moonpool, I know I am going."

"Goodbye old friend."

With that he breathed his last and he was gone. And because he was gone so was I.

Ban's blood still flowed in Bleddyn and his people so all I could do was watch and wait and hope.

Chapter 43

Fading

The earth rolled on and on, the seasons came and went, no one sought me. I began to hear of the new power that had risen above the others, a people who made nothing themselves but copied from others and were very efficient at doing so. They were a people who set their eyes on the world in order to make their own land great, a cruel, hard people.

I stood in the sanctuary under the full Moon. The air was still and I could hear the quiet movement of the night animals, the gentle rippling of the river. I breathed the smells of the soil and the grass and the leaves.

"Someone must believe in me again." I said to myself.

"I'm sorry, Moonpool, it is me." Arianrhod was standing by me. She seemed so very sad.

"What is this? Why have you called me?"

"Make the most of this, Moonpool, this may be our last chance to meet in human form."

"I don't understand. I know people have changed, but do they really not need us anymore?"

"It is not the people. You know that The Maker Of All Things has a particular interest to a people way out to the east."

"I have heard of them."

"He has always had a plan that involves them, he has given them messages over the ages and now it is getting close."

I said nothing, I had no idea what was coming.

"You know of the new power that is taking over much of the world from a place called Rome."

"Yes, I know our people have traded with them."

"The Maker Of All Things is about to reveal his plan to his chosen people and this new power will be the means the message is spread."

"And how does this affect us?"

"One of The Maker's messengers is soon to visit a young girl of his chosen people. He is planning to be born into the world."

"The Maker Of All Things? Born into the world?" I was stunned.

"Yes. And he will be also a fully human being, something even when we take on mortality we can never be, and he will do this while being The Maker Of All things at the same time."

"If he is coming to earth he is taking full control, he won't need us then."

"Lleu and I are saying goodbye while we can just in case this is so." She said. "Gabriel will visit her within the next rotation of the earth. Then The Spirit Of The Maker will cause her to conceive and at that moment the two worlds become one."

We embraced for a moment in silence. Then she had to move on. I concentrated hard to hold on to my physical form for as long as I could while I looked around for possibly the last time at the valley, the hills, the woods, the fields, the human shelters. But I could not hold on long.

I watched as the people woke and began to go about their daily business. Many of them started walking the land checking on the livestock. Those up in Pôl Mawr pulling fresh pots from the kilns, a new design again deeper and narrower. The cows were being milked. Grain was ground by the new mill up the valley to the north and new bread being baked. The blacksmith in Pentreban was firing up his forge. The pots of meat boiling on the stone built stoves and the vegetables being prepared. The warriors practicing with their new iron swords and iron tipped spears. Even now I could still feel the burning in my arm. The horses were being made ready for riding. Repairs were being made to the carts and one of the ploughs.

Then it happened. I felt the shock run through the whole of nature, The Son Of The Maker was conceived in woman and He was come to earth. And the humans were all blissfully unaware. But I was still here.

If I was still here perhaps I had until he was born, in which case I would see a summer and an autumn and the beginning of a winter.

I made the most of what time I had left. I played with the children as they were young enough still to hear my voice even if I could not appear. I ran with them invisibly through the long summer days and sometimes almost felt they caught a glimpse of my shadow in the shade of the trees or in the slowly rippling waters of a stream. The dogs and the horses could always see me and would turn towards me to the bafflement of the people.

In the autumn as the leaves fell I kicked them into the air and ran through them so my form could be discerned for a moment and when the mist filled the valley I caused it to swirl about me. People would see and maybe wonder for a moment but dismiss what they thought they saw and get on with their business.

Owain, their druid celebrated the equinox with them as had always been the custom. He was a good man and as he lit the sacred flame on the altar he declared. "This is for you, Pwll'euad." Yet he wasn't sure enough of my existence to see me. I had become a legend again, a story.

The earth rolled on and on, the days shortened, the weather was wet and cold. On the solstice Owain brought the people together again and they chanted and sang for the Sun to rise again and when he rose in a clear sky and his rays streamed across the sanctuary the people cheered and afterwards celebrated again as they always had.

And then it happened. The Son Of The Maker Of All Things was born. The messengers gathered on the hillside above his birthplace and sang to the humble shepherds. I felt the joy that The Maker had brought the two worlds together again and if this was my last moment then I knew it was worth it. I wanted to shout to the people here too but it was not my place. This was the beginning of the age when the human race must spread the news, when they must listen directly to The Maker Of All Things and our role was over.

I waited, but I am still here, I am still the valley and I am still Moonpool.

Lightning Source UK Ltd.
Milton Keynes UK
UKHW011849240921
391141UK00001B/34

9 781839 758171